Sslits

Michael Vance

AIRSHIP 27 PRODUCTIONS

SSLITS
© 2017 Michael Lail

Published by Airship 27 Productions
www.airship27.com
www.airship27hangar.com

Interior illustrations © 2017 Gary Kato
Cover illustration © 2017 Ted Hammond

Editor: Ron Fortier
Associate Editor: Fred Adams Jr.
Marketing and Promotions Manager: Michael Vance
Production and design by Rob Davis

ISBN-10:1-946183-17-2
ISBN-13: 978-1-946183-17-0

Printed in the United States of America

10 9 8 7 6 5 4 3 2 1

For the sake of clarity, the two alien beings in this novel have been given names. Their species is called Sslits; this designation is used as the personal name of one of the aliens. These creatures have no concept of time, space, individualism or singleness. They are a Hive that acts and communicates with one "mind" similar to ants, or birds flocking, or turtles creating furrows in the sands as they travel to the sea.

PROLOGUE

The enormous, elongated yellow city/mound was a bloated vein on the surface of the hard, cracked, and cratered sand that stretched to an immense distance in every direction.

Above the mound, the air shimmered from the intense heat of three red suns in an otherwise cloudless, pale green sky. Around it stretched huge fields of brown fungi so brittle that it would crumble at the touch of a hand. But there was no hand on the desert planet K'hupric.

There was no breeze, no vegetation, no birds or insects.

K'hupric was eerily silent except for the infrequent ululation of the Sslits on pilgrimage—like the moan of whales underneath the pale green oceans of Earth Seven—or a sudden and intense eruption *fawoooosh* from one of its thousands of craters that pockmarked the endless desert, sending a geyser of yellow sand that rose, rose, rose and mushroomed, and then rained dust back to the barren wilderness.

As was true every day, and as the suns sank below the horizon, six Sslits slowly sloshed across the sand at the foot of the eastern most end of their city/mound. Like gigantic slugs or snails, each of the red bags of squirming, communal maggots wore a ridged carapace made of its own 'flesh' over its back against the searing heat. Each of the monstrous things at one of the corners of what looked like a sled was pushing that flat disk across the sand towards a brown patch of fungi. Their advance to the harvest seemed to take forever; time was an unknown concept on K'hupric. The Sslits and the sled left shallow furrows behind them in the sand.

From that sled at its left and right sides hung oval shaped tools—small, woven, metal nets used as scoops in harvest. In its center lay strands of black metal twisted into a fat licorice. It was the Sslits' only weapon against their greatest foe and only fear, the ravenous, blind garbitch.

When the sled was finally in place at the edge of the fungi, these nets were laboriously removed from it using two appendages ending in two pronged pinchers that sprouted out from each of the sluggish creatures. So began the slow task for the red bags of mucous of *tic tic tic* chipping off chunks of the fungi and loading it onto the sled.

Their concentration was intense. They never heard the gigantic garbitch behind them as the monstrous thing slithered silently—a third of its worm's body raised up to strike—across the parched sand. Its immense mouth in the center of its blind head and its bear's trap of razor sharp teeth, the hundreds of writhing feelers used to smell, to feel, to snatch, to stuff Sslits down its cavernous craw were perfectly suited to capture each drop of liquid, utterly priceless because water was life and almost none existed on K'hupric outside of each gelatinous, communal body of each K'huprician.

K'hupric had not always been a planet that was no more than a blister on a cosmic furnace, a world of nothing but cracked earth; no oceans or streams or ponds or puddles, never clouds heavy with rain. The worldwide drought caused by its suns burning off most of its atmosphere had taken countless centuries to mar the planet forever. Life there had had much time to adapt or perish.

When it was within striking distance, the garbitch belched and sloshed within its skin.

As one, the six Sslits heard and turned. They screamed without mouths.

There was no hope—it was too late—but all but one of the Sslits stampeded, scattered out from the horror in all directions in what was slow motion to the garbitch.

Like a cobra, the garbitch *snap* struck, snatched up a Sslits in its slobbering jaws and, raising its head vertical to the rest of its body, jerked open its jaws. The feelers of the garbitch stuffed the screaming Sslits partially down its gaping maw, the Sslits torn to shreds by the garbitch's double row of teeth as it did so. The garbitch clamped its jaws down, and the Sslits's carapace was crushed and its body *pop* exploded like a ripe grape, and the juice of the Sslits trickled down the garbitch's throat and out of the corner's of its jaws to fall in spatter-shaped puddles on the cracked earth below.

The one Sslits that had not fled dredged the twist of licorice up and out of the bottom of the sled. Raising it carefully, it patted the top of the licorice

pat

pat

pat

Three times with its temporary limb.

A pencil thin, searing ray of yellow light *KAZATAZTAZT* instantly shot out of its tip.

A big chunk of the garbitch's raised left side *pfffuf* exploded, splattering on the cracked, parched earth, splattering on the Sslits holding its weapon.

The garbitch jerked its massive head vertical to its writhing body and screamed and screamed and screamed.

It was then that the siren atop the city/mound meant to warn of an approached garbitch was set off by a sentinel on the top of the mound that had witnessed the beginning of carnage below it. The siren was much too little, and much too late.

The weird ululation of the siren joined the screams of the garbitch.

The scream of the siren continued as the horror struck again, snatching up the Sslits by the shed in its slobbering jaws and, again raising its head vertical to the rest of its body, jerked open its jaws. The Sslits dropped its weapon to the sand below as it partially sunk down into the garbitch's jaws, torn to shreds as it did so. The garbitch clamped down, and the carapace cracked open and its body *pop* exploded like a grape, and its juices poured down the garbitch's gullet.

And as the garbitch fed, a silver disc soundlessly shot up from the western most edge of the city/mound at horrendous speed to blink out of sight into the sky.

CHAPTER ONE
THURSDAY, OCTOBER 5TH, 1944, 2:00 PM.
UNIVERSITY OF OKLAHOMA, NORMAN, OKLAHOMA
EARTH

Eric Gaines was sweating bullets in his rented suit. It was pinstriped.

The explosion of needless clichés in his mind hung motionless like confetti in the chilled air where he stood: the university chapel, the pastor who had been randomly found in a phone book, the chapel organist and the uncanny echo of the Wedding March, Celeste Jones and her elaborate and inappropriately *white* wedding dress, the Maid of Honor and two bridesmaids in outlandish pastel gowns, Eric's best man and two bridegrooms, all in cheap suits, the Bible, the candles, the light falling through stained glass windows, the musky, scented flowers and the drone of their vows spoken in unnaturally hushed tones, the polite kiss and the unspoken hunger.

As these disparaging thoughts ran like mice through Eric's mind, the weird and oddly inappropriate chords of the novelty song *Mairzy Doates* followed him and his bride, Celeste, from the organ down the aisle to the outside door of the chapel. Celeste was biting the manicured and polished fingernail of the first digit of her left hand

Eric Gaines hated clichés and rituals; he had always despised them. He knew instinctively that none of these mundane, man-made rituals would have any lasting impact on their marriage, positively or negatively. *But what else would one expect a bloodless, dyed-in-the-wool scientist specializing in mathematics to think?* He thought.

Eric also knew that his bride-to-be would not have had one of these worn and outdated chestnuts ignored and still agreed to marry him.

The chapel doors flung open and *Mairzy Doates* followed him and Celeste out as this fuzzy collage of almost unconscious impressions flashed through Eric's conflicted mind.

His one conscious thought was that he wanted sex.

He glanced over at his tom-boyishly beautiful wife and said, "I'm the luckiest man alive."

Eric knew it was true. At best, he was average. He had brown hair and eyes, an unremarkable complexion, and was of average height, weight and body build. He looked like a manikin in a department store window. The only thing exceptional was his mind.

He dimly heard laughter and chatter from the sparse wedding crowd lined up on both sides of the descending chapel stairs as his invisible explosion of clichés became a visible rain of thrown rice and confetti. Gaines and his bride ran out of the chapel's double doors stooped over with their heads bowed and protected by their hands. He imagined they looked like the famous painting of Adam and Eve being driven from the Garden of Eden except there was no angel with a flaming sword denying them reentry. It just felt to Eric like they were being driven into an uncertain future together.

As he and Celeste descended the steps, a beat up old 1934 Chevy Master Sedan with faded blue paint waited for them at the curb. Her father had given the car to her as a wedding gift. The clichéd *just married* was scrawled with soap across its back window, and the typical train of empty tin cans were tied to the back bumper. At that moment, Eric could not know that Celeste Jones' own fuzzy thoughts were of three things that were incomprehensibly one and paradoxically almost universally central to all lives of all women:

Security. Family. Children.

Oh, Mairzy doats and dozy doats and little lambsy divey

A kiddley divey, too. Wouldn't you?

As Eric and his bride ran the gauntlet of family and friends, trying to beat the rice away with his open hand, Eric again glanced to his left at the twenty eight year old farm girl, six years his senior, from tiny, rural Byng, Oklahoma who wore an expression of focused indifference and who looked for all the world like a hood ornament on an Edsel—the smooth, heart-shaped flawless face and short blond bob of the famous female pilot, Amelia Earhart. That face, free of any cosmetics, not even lipstick, was nothing like his own completely forgettable mug that couldn't be remembered unless one had seen it at least six or seven times—and thought *but what else would a woman and a bloodless, dyed-in-the-wool scientist specializing in forensics think?*

That's when he saw the white tear in the outside corner of her left eye pucker and ball and then break free and begin to crawl down her cheek to her chin.

As Eric watched it crawl, he continued to try to beat the thrown rice away with his open hand, but his clenched fist came back full of the stuff.

That's when he knew that the white tear was not white and was not a tear.

It was a maggot.

Still hunched over, he opened his hand. He looked at his opened hand.

It wasn't full of rice.

It was full of maggots.

"Haah?!"

Eric jerked up in bed, his face beaded with sweat. He was breathing heavily. The sheets were sweaty and twisted around his body.

He said, "Holy God," which was appropriate since he, not Celeste, was the one who still believed in God.

He looked at the radio sitting by the clock on the bed stand that he'd left on for white noise. It was whispering: *Oh, Mairzy doats and dozy doats and little lambsy divey; A kiddley divey, too. Wouldn't you?*

Eric looked at the clock.

Again, he said, "Holy God!"

It was obvious to Eric in hindsight that he had drunk, danced, and sang too much at his bachelor party. He would have cursed himself for being so out of character and so stupid if it would have done any good.

So he shook the nightmare and the song out of his head, and got up out of bed.

After all, Eric Gaines had no time for this kind of animalist nonsense. He only had three hours left to get dressed for his wedding.

CHAPTER TWO
WEDNESDAY, JULY 2, 3:31PM, 1947

A gent Celeste Gaines did not see the explosion in the sky.

Hurtling at blinding speed, the flying saucer punched a hole through the atmosphere of earth over the Atlantic Ocean. Having instantly shattered the sound barrier and wobbling from the impact, the superheated silver disc measuring fifty-two feet across roared dozens of miles above and over the vast body of water, always descending foot by foot. Its white hot backwash of raw power freckled with black energy clots vaporized every fleck of organic and nonorganic matter in its path.

Celeste was in New Mexico and did not see it. No ship of any tonnage saw it either as it screamed across the sky. No radar tracked it. No sailor raised his face to the sky. At the mouth of the Hudson River and the stem of the Big Apple—the city thrown like building blocks along the shore of the river—not one of the tens of thousands of New Yorkers crawling like a swarm of ants in the elevated trains and skyscrapers, in the subways, and cramming its streets and sidewalks, gave the unseen flying saucer a moment's thought as it slowed to eleven thousand miles an hour.

Celeste was taking out the trash in her clandestine CIA office when the space ship blinked into the range of human sight, a black smudge in the cerulean blue sky, far behind the skirts of the massive, copper, Statue of Liberty. It was outlined by the statue's raised arm and torch and the helmet on her head for less than the blink of an eye.

In a nanosecond, it and its searing backwash were framed by two of the huge, metal spikes of the statue's spiked helmet.

In a second nanosecond, the saucer hurtled over Liberty's massive shoulder.

In another nanosecond, it swept past Liberty's helmet.

The tiny tourists inside and peering intently out of its thick plate glass windows, wide-eyed and awed by New York City's jumble of concrete skyscrapers, were oblivious to the horrendous descent of the alien craft except for one five year old girl in a flowered dress.

She grabbed her mother's skirt with her left hand, and with her right hand, pointed out of the window at the saucer.

Excited, she said, "Lookee, lookee, mommy. I see a saucer!!"

Her mother ignored her.

It was 1947, and the Cold War with Russia was escalating and festering and the fear of an Atomic Armageddon and the End of Days was spreading across America, and movies about giant bugs created by radioactivity were lighting up movie screens. Although paranoia turned many eyes and ears to the sky that day for these and other reasons, at seven thousand miles an hour, no one heard it scream.

At the time that it fell across the sky, Celeste was low "man" in the tiny CIA office in distant New Mexico.

In its erratic flight, no one even saw its shadow as it, second by second, slowed to four thousand miles an hour, blocking out the sun across Pennsylvania and Ohio, three thousand miles an hour as it scattered random cloud formations over Indiana, two thousand miles an hour over the cloudless skies of Illinois and Missouri and, at five hundred miles an hour, shearing off the topmost trees of the tallest mountain in Oklahoma.

If one person or device had seen or captured its image that day, mankind would have learned that man is not the only image of God.

Celeste would be the first to learn.

•••

Agent Celeste Gaines would only learn about the initial incursion of the flying saucer and what followed its crash years later. It was not a surprise. After all, the Central Intelligence Agency of which she was an employee at the time had always been exceptional at piecing together a story...after the fact.

In the heart of a violent thunderstorm veined with lightning over Corona, New Mexico, the scream of the crippled flying saucer shuddered in an explosive thunderclap.

The now fireball plummeted five hundred feet through the heavy clouds, wind and rain. It nicked the skin of the desert.

It struck again and again, skipping across the ground, chewing out huge chunks of sand, rock, and cacti, and belching it out in a cloud of debris behind it as the saucer began to break apart. It bellowed and spat desert debris and small, superheated parts of itself over miles of desert.

It plowed a red hot gash in the earth for almost half a mile until it lurched to a stop, throwing up a shallow crater around it, and ended its long journey across the galaxy, motionless in the arid land around Corona, New Mexico.

As it struck, heads did rise and ears were turned up as far away as Lincoln, Ruidoso and Artesia, New Mexico as a few ranchers and farmers and homemakers staring out bedroom windows at the overcast sky were watching for approaching thunderstorms near them.

At his ranch house near Corona where the storm raged, sheep rancher Max Brazel heard the impact which he would later describe as a "megaton" explosion in his pasturage. He used the word not because he understood it, but because he liked how it sounded and also because he had led somewhat of a solitary life and had dropped out of school in the middle of the Eighth Grade but liked to talk a lot down at the barber shop when he got his thinning hair cut.

As the flying saucer gouged the desert, sand was thrown up and behind it and was caramelized in chocolate brown ridges like marshmallows seared by fire.

Then the scream died.

•••

Early on the morning of July 3rd, Agent Celeste Gaines opened the front door of *Mid-Continent Insurance and Casualty* in Roswell, New Mexico.

Early on the same morning, Max Brazel found the flying saucer's corpse.

He drove his 1937 Ford half-ton Highboy gingerly out to check his pasturage because the old pickup truck was held together by spit and bailing wire. Max was not a wealthy man.

When he reached the crater, he got out of the pickup, not really expecting anything unusual in a life that had been mundane, at best, and took off his cowboy hat, slapped it against his left thigh, scratched his head with his free hand, and said, "What the hell...?!?"

That was a big deal because Max was a quiet, soft-spoken man who seldom cursed.

The debris field was huge, and the metal fragments looked odd. He picked up some small pieces of it using his handkerchief to protect his hands from the heat, threw them in the bed of his truck, and drove to a neighbor who lived close by. That neighbor scratched his own head after looking at the debris and advised Max to call the police.

Max called the police. The sheriff's name was Wilcox, and it took a long time for Brazel to convince Wilcox to come take a look because Wilcox thought Brazel was nuts.

The sheriff *didn't* believe him, but Wilcox sent one of his policemen to follow Max from his house out to the wreckage only because it was a very slow, boring day.

The policeman didn't have a clue about much of anything in life much less of what he saw, and told Brazel to call an office in Roswell and gave him the phone number.

The woman who answered on the other end of the line, Celeste Gaines, lived to regret answering the phone that day. By the time she was twelve years old, it had been obvious that she would grow up to be a blond, blue-eyed, comely but not beautiful girl of average height and weight and figure. By the time she was sixteen, she had become the American ideal of the girl next door. But no one had ever thought that, when a mother of a two-year-old daughter and a one-year-old son, she would be an agent of the CIA stationed in a backwater burg in New Mexico pretending to be a secretary at an insurance company.

Max said, "Hello, my name is Max Brazel, and I heared this huge explosion last night and found this big thing in the back forty of my pasture this morning, and nobody seems to know what it is. Sheriff said I should call you."

Celeste Gaines said, "Why me?"

"It perty much barbequed four head of my sheep where they stood."

Celeste leaned forward just an inch or two in her chair behind her desk in the Spartan little God-forsaken clandestine CIA office under the guise of *Mid-Continent Insurance* where she had worked at a position barely two steps above receptionist.

She said, "Well, get yourself a fork and have lunch!"

She waited for laughter, but heard none.

Brazel continued, "This thing looks like one of them flyin' saucers I seen at the drive-in movies, and it's buried in the ground with its butt stuck up in the air. There's junk everywhere. It's super hot and it kinda glows. I started sweatin' just walkin' towards it."

"Sir," asked Celeste, "is it possible that you've been...drinking?"

CHAPTER THREE

On July 8th, Celeste and three military men from Roswell's Air Force Base drove the long, dusty, and mostly empty road to Max's pasture on what each though was a stupid, time wasting, wild goose chase.

What Celeste and the three men saw left them speechless and astonished. They sat for at least ten minutes in their vehicle before even thinking of dressing in their containment suits and stepping out into the vast, uncanny crater.

The huge, silver, flying saucer, in some measure smeared with dirt, was partially buried in the bank of dirt it had thrown up when it had crashed. Little glints of light reflecting the sun randomly flashed on its skin where that highly polished surface was dirt free. A third of the alien craft was embedded up to the edge of its shallow, cracked dome in its center. The teeth of that circular dome looked like the mid-span supports, or blades, in a jet engine. At the bottom of the dome was an open wound in the shattered blades.

The bulk of the flying saucer jutted at a thirty-three degree angle up and out of the earth.

Despite the dust that hung in the air that would make breathing difficult for Celeste and her team, it seemed to glow.

The sand around the alien vessel had been cauterized into scalloped glass. Three thin, greenish-purple wisps of smoke rose lazily from three smaller, additional wounds in its skin on its outer edge. Glimpses of the inexplicable bones of the craft inside were visible under the wounds. The acrid odor of what smelled most like raw sewage permeated the air.

Shocked and awed into silence, Celeste and the men continued to study the wreckage as they slowly donned bulky radiation suits inside the van that was parked about two hundred yards from the ship.

Three of the Air Force men, finally dressed in their suits with one slowly waving the wand of his Geiger counter in the still air, were already cautiously approaching the saucer as Celeste Gaines zipped up the last zipper on her suit and picked up her Geiger counter from the seat of their vehicle.

One of the men was snapping photographs with a camera.

Little emotion showed on her face, but that was deceptive. This was the single most startling event in her life, challenging and already shattering much of what she had learned and believed in with unquestioning certainty as a scientist up to that moment. But Celeste had learned early in her career that deadpan expressions were standard gear for scientists.

She unconsciously touched the name badge of her suit above her left breast—it read GAINES—slipped her protective helmet over her head, and stepped out of the van. Although sound was muffled by her helmet, she heard and noted that the ground underneath her boots crunched as she walked.

One of the three men, Lieutenant Toren Walker, stopped short of the alien craft by about twenty yards and simply stared in utter disbelief. He carried a tape recorder by a strap over the shoulder of his suit. His broad, somewhat flat face, framed both by his heavy, black glasses and the protective window in his helmet, was almost rigid. His concentration was so focused that, when he raised the microphone of his recorder to capture any available sound, he accidentally and clumsily struck his own name plate with it. His completely human response was to glance quickly about to see if his fellows had seen him do so; lieutenants are not supposed to be clumsy. When he saw Celeste so far behind them, he waved her forward with a heavily gloved hand and waited impatiently for her to catch up to him. He did so because, at that time, no device existed that would let them communicate with each other while in their protective radiation suits.

When they had all reached the formidable, yawning wound in the lower quadrant of the dome, it was Walker who waved Celeste and the other two men forward.

The airman and Celeste both glanced at their Geiger counters again, and were relieved when they saw that their devices did not register radioactivity. Then, all of them overcome with trepidation, they slowly and guardedly entered the gaping hole with some effort.

In a matter of minutes, Celeste found herself walking down a perfectly smooth, circular hallway that seemed to constantly and endlessly curve away from her and deeper into the ship. It was impossible for her to tell if the walls were organic or inorganic. They were made of something… unearthly. The hall was well lit but by no discernible source of light. The oppressive heat on the skin of the craft was absent from its bowels and the eerie silence inside of the saucer was broken only by the sound of the footfalls of Celeste's team.

When she and her three explorers finally came to a fork in the tube, they took the hallway on their right that seemed to curve further into the center of the craft.

It did.

After several tense moments, that hall opened onto…

Celeste dropped the wand of her Geiger counter that swung, forgotten, at her side as her face contorted with disbelief and horror.

Behind her and to her left side, the airman with the camera retched inside the helmet of his containment suit.

Using his left arm to brace himself, Lieutenant Toren Walker fell sideways against the tube's wall.

Celeste later wrote in her first report to the Central Intelligence Agency chiefs that the four had entered what appeared to be an alien cockpit. It would prove to be exactly that.

Squashed into the concave, metal, pilot's seat in the middle of the cockpit was an unspeakable alien horror.

A confusing chaos of tubes or wires, some probably electrical, some dripping with ochre, some with a type of metallic shielding, ran from the walls of the flying saucer to the body of that horror. Of varying lengths and widths, a few were attached by a metallic band around the thing's middle. Some of the tubing was directly attached to the slimy blob.

The intense alien odor was overpowering.

Many years later, Celeste wrote that her first impression was of an immense, mostly transparent placenta sack filled with nauseating mucus.

The amorphous body of the noxious alien monster was throbbing.

It was on that day that Celeste Gaines, Toren Walker, and two other unidentified airmen learned that man is not the only creature made in the image of God.

The team later learned that they weren't from Mars.

They weren't little and they weren't green.

The bag of writhing maggots in the concave chair was blood red.

CHAPTER FOUR

As they worked into the early morning hours of July 9th, the New Mexico sunrise painted streaks of sherbet just above the horizon. The original four at the site, including Celeste, and a large contingency of support personnel from the Air Force base who had frantically brought with them a massive crane, excavator, and several flat-bed trucks, had cordoned off the crash site, scooped up the debris, removed the saucer and everything in it with every scrap of evidence.

Eventually, they would even sweep the sand clean of tire tracks.

It had been a herculean task made even more difficult since everyone wore radiation suits. However, considering the consequences of not scrubbing the site—world-wide panic and chaos—every drop of sweat, every stubbed toe, every strained muscle, every profanity whispered under someone's breath, was more than worth it.

Because she was the local forensic expert for the CIA, it was just assumed, although unspoken, that she was somehow responsible for the oversight, preservation, and transportation of the one horrific alien blob that at least seemed on the surface to be throbbing with life.

The site wasn't the only thing that needed scrubbing in the coming days.

The policeman who had been brought to the site by Max earlier was located by Celeste and sworn to silence for the sake of National Security, and under the threat of much more than just the loss of his job. Max Brazel and the neighbor he first approached were sworn to silence by the CIA operatives that quickly joined Celeste in Roswell. The promise of a large sum of money was given to guarantee their silence.

It didn't work, and neither Max nor his neighbor ever got the money. So the need to fabricate what 'really happened' from whole cloth was almost immediate.

On the same day, Roswell's newspaper reported the discovery of the wreckage of a huge flying saucer and that, four miles away and several days later, the bodies of four dead aliens had also been found.

By 6 p.m. that day, Brigadier General Roger Ramey, although Toren Walker wrote it, issued a press release and photograph claiming the wreckage was a weather balloon. A wise man for his age, Ramey had an eye on his pension and retirement. Walker was twenty-five years old at the time, still wet behind the ears, and still one-hundred percent sold on American Exceptionalism and was rock-solid in his patriotism. He would have set himself on fire if ordered to do so.

So, denied its panic, the vast majority of the people of the world eventually went back to eating and sleeping and working, buying and selling and trading and stealing, completely oblivious to possibly the greatest single event in the history of the world.

Over the years, Roswell's Flying Saucer became little more than an urban legend, a cottage industry, the subject of several lunatic-fringe books and television specials, and the object of derision by reasonable people everywhere...as was intended.

Brazel. Weather Balloons. Dead little green men.
It was all a lie.

•••

The actual events that immediately followed before Max's interview with a local radio station reporter named Frank Joyce, before Joyce's report to the Roswell Army Air Force Base's Intelligence Officer, Jesse Marcel Sr., and Marcel's visit to the site and his own harvesting of debris were known by very few people. Under the careful manipulation of the military, it became the stuff of rumor, then a joke, then a shame, then snowballed into a cover up and a conspiracy theory, and then finally became a world-wide obsession—the actual events were never reported by anyone to anyone in the public realm.

Celeste Gaines was only among the first to make certain that they were never reported.

On Sunday, July 6th, 1947, little unassuming, honest-to-a-fault, Max Brazel had driven seventy-five miles into the town of Roswell.

And into history.

Max didn't drive into history because he'd happened to chance upon a weather balloon or a two-seater airplane crumpled up in the middle of a still smoking crater.

The five aliens, four of them dead, were real.

CHAPTER FIVE
SATURDAY, AUGUST 18, 1923,
CHESSER'S GROCERIES AND GAS, BYNG, OKLAHOMA

By the time of the crash, Celeste Jones Gaines was already a mass of contradictions held in stasis in separate little compartments buried deep in her mind, as is true of every human being. She was becoming a bit complicated even when she was a little girl in pigtails that were bleached blond from working in the sun. She had been wearing worn and patched overalls at seven years old, going on eight.

Celeste was born on Monday, Oct. 30th, 1916, at 11:16 p.m. in her parents' house in Byng, Oklahoma. At the time, sparsely populated Byng was a farming and ranching community about five miles north of the much larger town of Ada. Ada had a teachers college, East Central, and was the largest town in a thirty mile radius with a population of eight thousand four hundred and fifty seven.

Celeste was the only child ever born into her family.

Celeste's hometown of Byng had a school that was one of two centers of the rural social life of the otherwise isolated community. It drew students for all twelve grades from a large area. It also had several automobile repair shops, a taxidermist and butcher working out of his home who mounted and dressed the deer seasonally killed by Byng's hunters, and Chesser's Groceries and Gas. Chesser's was located at the intersection of the dirt road that also ran by Celeste's home and a paved, two lane, state highway. Byng also was the home of five small Christian churches.

Celeste's parents were hard working farmers who unquestionably believed in God, family, and country, and Celeste was raised as a Christian even before she knew what the word meant in the First (Southern) Baptist Church of Byng, membership fifty two. Their church was the second social center of the Joneses otherwise labor-intensive and dreary life. Pot-luck, church-wide dinners—a feast of pies, fried chicken, ham, green beans, corn and mashed potatoes—were a highlight of the Jones' church life.

Celeste's early years were spent working with her father, feeding the pigs and a constantly changing number of chickens each day in the morning. She also fed two cows and a horse. The Jones' thought of these animals as utilitarian. Celeste also helped her mother clean house and make supper.

They made their living from growing cotton.

Her home had no electricity, no indoor bathroom, and water was pumped from a well in the backyard into the kitchen sink. The Joneses owned no radio, and the only book in the house was a Bible that her father read to Celeste just before bedtime each night. After each reading, her father gently hugged her with his rock-hard arms and kissed her on the forehead.

As he tucked her under the quilt, he would always say, "Don't forget to thank the Lord for all of our blessings, little buttercup."

Celeste liked being called buttercup.

Her mother would then quietly pad her way into Celeste's tiny bedroom and lavish her daughter with love.

The nearest house was a half mile from her own very modest and isolated home, and the elderly couple who lived there had no children. But

Celeste was completely happy because she knew of no other lifestyle except in the comic strips in the newspapers that her father occasionally brought home. Celeste's dad read them all to her, over and over again—*Mutt and Jeff*, *Out Our Way*, *Boots* and others. *Moon Mullins* was her favorite in the *Ada Evening News*.

These were the routines and rituals and family and friends that were the core of Celeste's understanding of life until she left for college.

They were all thrown into question by the flying saucer.

One of her greatest joys in her simple seven years of life was her black, white, and brown, short-haired, mongrel dog, Mitsy. She loved Mitsy with all of her young heart and with no less an intimate love than she gave to her father and mother.

Celeste and Misty were inseparable. Mitsy trailed after her as she did her outside daily chores, and cavorted with her as she acted out her fantasies after her chores were done with found sticks as swords and rocks for cannon balls and tiny forts made of mud. Sitting at Celeste's feet at table, Mitsy ate with the Jones family three times a day, every day. Celeste couldn't keep her hands off of her, and petted her best friend frequently. Mitsy slept at the foot of Celeste's bed every night.

She called Mitsy "unhuman" despite her parents correcting her because she didn't think of Mitsy as an animal and didn't know another word that fit and was certain that adding un to the front of any word gave a word an opposite meaning. Mom and Pop didn't object too long because it was just "too darn cute" when she said it.

Celeste often talked openly to her unhuman friend as if Mitsy was her sister. As far as Mitsy was concerned, she was Celeste's sister.

That is why Saturday, August 18, 1923, almost killed Celeste and did far worse for Mitsy.

As part of her early years, her father paid the towheaded tomboy the outrageous sum of a nickel a week each Saturday for her work, and Celeste spent that coin on a fistful of candy from Chesser's Groceries and Gas. Her favorites were Double Bubble chewing gum, Hershey's Kisses, Bit O Honey candy bars, and Black Crows.

The last time she would ever buy any of them was on that day.

On that warm, dry, August morning, Celeste paused on her long trek to Chesser's to spend her nickel and waved goodbye to Mitsy who sat in front of their Craftsman house. Mitsy instantly jumped up, wagged her tail, and barked. But Celeste's best friend in the whole wide world was not allowed to make the trip to the little grocery store with her. So Mitsy

" ... AS IF MISTY WAS
   HER SISTER. "

always waited patiently but with a broken heart in the Jones' front yard for *her* best friend's return home.

It was only a half mile walk on a dirt road seldom traveled by cars; not many of Celeste's neighbors owned any type of vehicle. It was also a road often walked by the little girl, so it seemed to her only moments had passed when she placed a hand on the Double Cola screen door push bar and swung the door of Chesser's open on a wonderland of delights.

As always, her's was a tough choice from among the dozens of sweet temptations. It demanded much time, but she eventually chose a handful of Hershey's Kisses.

Almost home, she couldn't delay eating a chocolate drop any longer, took one out of her little brown sack, and unwrapped it. A 1914 Chevrolet Series L4d Touring Car held together with spit and faith was limping down the road some distance behind her.

The instant Mitsy saw "buttercup", she jumped up and trotted out to meet her.

Celeste was biting the fingernail of the first digit of her left hand. She saw her best friend and smiled broadly and waved that hand in greeting.

Mitsy ran out and onto the highway.

Celeste leaned forward at the waist and called out, "Here girl, here girl, here girl!"

The Chevy was only ten feet or so behind Celeste, pulling into the opposite lane to pass the girl when she waved.

Mitsy ran toward Celeste and in front of the Chevy.

Now also seeing the car, Celeste screamed, "MITSY!!!" and lurched forward.

The car swerved to avoid hitting Celeste.

Mitsy moved into the new path of the car.

There was a heavy thud.

As the 1914 Chevrolet Series L4d Touring Car sped away, Celeste screamed, "Mitsy!!" again as she fell to her knees in front of the broken bones, bloody fur, heaving chest, and fading whimper that was left behind.

Celeste rocked back and forth as she cradled Mitsy's bloody head in her lap, sobbing. Mitsy was panting heavily and Celeste could hear an unnatural gurgle in her dog's throat.

Then Mitsy's life seeped out in red tears until her ruptured heart stopped beating and her chest stopped heaving and her beautiful black eyes glazed over.

Mitsy shuddered and died.

And the uncodified, subconscious, but core belief of Celeste in the absolute, unchanging certainly of everything she knew about the world was shattered, and what had been at most a cautionary fairy tale—incomprehensible Death—became brutal reality.

As Celeste sobbed uncontrollably, stroking Mitsy's sticky, matted fur, and holding Mitsy's corpse in her arms, she swore in her heart of hearts that no one would ever hurt another living thing again for as long as she lived.

Two days later, Celeste ate fried squirrel that her father had shot for supper.

CHAPTER SIX
2:15PM, THURSDAY, AUG. 29, 1946,
LOVELACE REGIONAL HOSPITAL, ROSWELL, NEW MEXICO

Celeste's left hand was a vise crushing her husband's right hand. Her unpolished fingernails were cutting little crescents of blood in his palm. Her blue eyes were clenched tightly shut. She moaned, "oh, oh, oh," but Eric said nothing in response. He wasn't stupid. He had learned something from the birth of their first child.

Her pain was so excruciating that Celeste had to bite her lower lip to keep from screaming. That left a smear of blood on her lower lip. Her teeth were clenched, and the muscles crawled around her jaw as another contraction hit her like a fist in the stomach.

"Try to think about the good times, you know, growing up," said Eric. "Remember how much you enjoyed the clubs you were active in when you were a little girl?"

Celeste moaned, "oh, oh, oh, oh."

"Remember the Future Farmers of America that you loved so much, honey?" Eric continued, ignoring the pain of her hand crushing his hand. "How you raised that bull from its birth in your senior year when you were all of seventeen and entered him in the State Fair in Oklahoma City and won the Grand Prize. That prize paid for most of your college. Remember, sweetie?"

She opened her blue, bloodshot eyes and looked up into Eric Gaines' average face, his mundane brown eyes, and his lackluster brown nondescript hair. At that moment, illogically and yet undeniably, Celeste knew that something important inside her had just died in room nine of the Lovelace Hospital.

It was not the child.

It was all true, of course, that she had excelled in all of her high school classes in Byng long ago and was promoted early twice. Celeste was a genius, a fact that had not gone unrecognized by her parents or her teachers or even by her husband. But being genius didn't amount to a hill of beans at the moment.

She said, "Listen moron, did you happen to notice I'm givin' birth to a baby here; your baby? Could you stop talkin' nons…oooooh!" and squeezed his hand again with a hand like an iron vise.

He told himself that it was the pain talking, but it did sting a bit. So he reminded himself that she was perfect, and she was his, and that was all that had mattered.

His opinion, however, was beginning to change.

In non sequitur after non sequitur, she thought that raising cattle hadn't prepared her much for this as she moaned, "Oh, oh, oh, oh," and that having grown up a 'loner' hadn't prepared her for childbirth, either.

Celeste had loved animals then as she did now. Indeed, she had always seemed more interested in animals than in her fellow classmates. She had never had any close friends, but never felt lonely. She was looked on by her fellow students as aloof, odd, and even snobbish.

Eric said, "That's it, baby; breathe, breathe, breathe."

She said, "Shut up, Eric!"

Her fellow classmates were right.

But none of that blocked the waves of pain that, apparently, were her reward for getting close enough to Eric to marry him.

Eric patted her hand and said, "But, honey, I'm just trying to help."

She looked up into her husband's face and something like disdain, disgust, even hatred seemed to burn in her eyes. She thought idiot but wasn't sure if she were describing him, herself, or both of them.

Out loud, she again said, "Shut up, Eric."

Eric shut up. It was a skill he had learned to do early in his marriage for that girl who wasn't average or normal.

Celeste had been the youngest girl to ever graduate from Byng, graduating Summa Cum Laude and winning a full scholarship to East Central State College, a teacher's college in nearby Ada where she had met Eric.

She had never been modest about her accomplishments, but oddly, never proud of them either. Celeste had also made in clear to anyone that would listen that there were two major events at East Central that had molded her life. The first was when she had stopped going to church and had decided that she didn't want to teach anything.

As Celeste groaned, "Ooh!" that didn't seemed to matter at the moment.

Excelling in the few science classes available at East Central, particularly biology, she had become dissatisfied with the small college and transferred after two years to the University of Oklahoma. They had welcomed their new genius with open arms at OU.

The second major event in her life stood up from the chair where he sat by her bed when her doctor and two nurses entered.

Eric had only mildly impressed her then. Although he was six years her junior in age, when they learned they had grown up so close to one another, they had become instant friends. That initial friendship was a surprise in Celeste. She was used to being ignored or feared by boys, especially one like Eric who had always been a social bee by nature.

It was then that her doctor entered and asked Eric to leave the room. He left.

As the door closed behind him, the memory of her marriage after a year of dating on Oct. 5, 1944 flashed across his mind. She was twenty-eight years old and he was twenty-two, and both had been quietly recruited by the CIA only six months after they were married.

She thought of their first job together working out of the same clandestine office in Oklahoma City. There, she had taken baby steps up through the ranks of the agency while Eric Gaines had risen through the ranks ahead of her.

She had not liked that.

Then suddenly and without explanation, they were both transferred to a satellite office, a hell-hole that was forsaken by both God and Man in Roswell, New Mexico.

She remembered Sept. 22, 1945, the day their first child had been born, when she had been twenty nine years old. Celeste had named her Margo. Now, their second and last child was being born even as Eric sat down on a bench in the hallway outside of his wife's room.

Eric had chosen to name the baby Richard if a boy and Elly if she was a girl. And as little Richard entered the world with little intermittent bouts of crying, Celeste took a deep breath, and closed her eyes.

She began to hallucinate.

Suddenly, somehow, and somewhere in the background, The Andrews Sisters were singing "Rum and Coca Cola". She knew that didn't make sense, but she listened anyway. It was her favorite song.

Disembodied, Celeste floated with the weight of a dandelion above a large, flat, rooftop on a skyscraper. It was surrounded by a ragged landscape of other skyscrapers of varying heights that stretched in every direction, fading from her sight into the horizon. Each of those buildings was a crossword puzzle of randomly lighted and dark windows.

From somewhere and nowhere, the sisters sang:

From Chicachicaree to Mona's Isle,
Native girls all dance and smile,
Help soldier celebrate his leave,
Make every day like New Year's Eve.

Celeste looked up. The sky was a splatter, a confetti of light, and a gibbous, pockmarked moon hung above her. It was deep night. Impossibly, and without moving from where she bobbed and floated above, she looked down the side of the building where a huge, fat, neon sign protruded from the skyscraper's facade, a number 1 that ran vertically down its entire length to the sidewalk far below. In raised lettering inside the number, but in much smaller letters, the words First National Bank blinked off and on, off and on, off and on.

Such a bank was completely unknown to her. Celeste looked back to the roof.

She saw herself lying on the roof, dead, in a brass coffin, her fish-belly white face and hands already beginning to shred as they decomposed. She was dressed in a white shroud with her hands crossed over her chest. Eric was standing next to the coffin dressed like a medieval executioner in a black hood. He was wielding a huge, double-edged axe. They both were at the foot of a large billboard elevated high above the rooftop on metal struts that read All The News That Fits above the image of a man reading the front page of a copy of the Global Star tabloid newspaper. Its headline read:

Maggot Love Child
Dies With Mother
By Ace Montana

Celeste watched Eric look at the billboard and then around himself at the skyscrapers.

He said, "No geese and ducks and surreys with a fringe on top. Tulsa looks a lot like my Memphis. And every other city I've been in."

As he said it, a goon in a domino mask and dressed in dirty clothes appeared in front of him at the base of the billboard. He carried a giant stick of black licorice across his forearms. It was Toren Walker with a face like a crumpled newspaper.

Pointing at the licorice, Eric said, "I am Eric Gaines. What in Hell is that?"

From somewhere and nowhere, the Andrews sisters sang: Drinkin' rum and Coca Cola, Go down Point Koomahnah, Both mother and daughter, Workin' for the Yankee dollar, Oh, you vex me, you vex me.

"Don' you watch th' tube?" sneered the thug. "This black baby kills!! This is th' bomb, man!! Five thou is cheap man; this is better than a freakin' nuclear weapon."

Then Toren grinned and added, "But you ain't seen nothing, yet," and took one step to his left side revealing the gigantic, pulsating, red maggot behind him.

Standing up on its slimy hindquarters, and with a mouth full of razor sharp teeth, it said, "Aah. Plenty of the damned for me to harvest and eat tonight. Maybe even greater evil here than usual...to have drawn me so far from home."

From her coffin, dead Celeste protested, "That thing is disgusting!"

Toren extended his arms, offering the licorice stick to Eric.

He said, "As you ordered, buckaroo. Cheap at any price."

The maggot burbled, "Today, Eric Gaines, you'll join your brothers in Hell."

Eric dropped his axe on the roof, accepted the licorice log, and studied it for a moment. The he pressed a trigger on the bottom of it. The licorice stick hummed to life in his hands, its power charging up.

He pointed the licorice stick at the thug and said, "I'm gonna blow yer head off, Toren!!"

Eric pulled the trigger. A pencil thin, searing ray of yellow light instantly shot out of its tip. The ray missed. It struck the billboard. The billboard evaporated.

Toren Walker turned, fled away down the roof, and jumped off; jumped up and flew away into the night sky.

From where she still floated above the roof, Celeste heard the dead Celeste say, "You can't kill someone who's already dead."

Eric aimed the licorice at the red maggot and pulled the trigger and a pencil thin ray of white-hot light shot out of its tip.

The maggot exploded in a cloud of tiny, squirming maggots that splattered on the billboard, splattered on Eric, that splattered on dead Celeste.

They fell with a sloppy noise like wet flour on the roof, squirming.

They fell as Celeste opened her eyes.

Lying in her bed in her hospital room, confused and frightened by her nightmare, Celeste began to cry.

On the bench outside her hospital room, Eric buried his face in his hands and wept.

Eric wept because he knew that something had just ended moments ago in room nine of the Lovelace Hospital.

His marriage had just died.

CHAPTER SEVEN

MONDAY, NOVEMBER 24, 1947, 9:30AM
ROSWELL AIR FORCE BASE, ROSWELL, NEW MEXICO

Lieutenant Toren Walker felt hot and on edgy as he sat in the little, windowless room usually used on the Roswell Air Force Base to interview new civilian employees. He was edgy because he was twenty-five years old and inexperienced, because he didn't know why he had been ordered to the room, and because he was both awed by and deeply afraid of "The Box," the nickname of Air Base Wing Commander Ralph Hinkle. He watched the closed metal door of the room like a cat stalking a bird as he twiddled with his regulation cap. It and nothing else was sitting on a small, metal table meant to seat four. He was sweating a bit, although it was November, and the summer heat of New Mexico had broken some time ago. So he took his handkerchief out of his breast pocket and wiped his flat face.

The lesser officers and enlisted men called Air Base Wing Commander Ralph Hinkle "The Box" because he looked like a stack of boxes barely restrained by his military uniform. They did not call him that to his face.

All jutting, hard-edged angles, and all about business and little else, he was not a man to elbow in the ribs as you sat in a bar lying about women, drinking beer, and telling the latest off-color joke.

The door swung open and, as he stepped briskly into the room, Commander Hinkle asked, "Where is Agent Celeste Gaines?"

Walker's mood darkened. Although he tried to hide it, there was little that he liked about the Central Intelligence Agency operative assigned to the monster secreted under one of the airfield's hangers. He didn't like it that she was only six years his senior but, in a sense, outranked him in the secret project he was sworn to protect. He didn't like it that she was obviously smarter than him, better looking as a woman than he was as a man, and a woman.

Hinkle closed the door and stepped into the room with the confidence of rank. He took off his hat and threw it on the table as he pulled back a metal chair from the table. He began to sit down.

As the commander did so, Walker said, "Mrs. Gaines wouldn't know how to read a watch if she had one, sir. My guess is that she's probably in front of and on her knees worshipping that alien bag of maggots, Commander Hinkle."

Hinkle stopped himself from sitting down. He stood half crouched, glaring at Walker for what seemed to the young officer like ten million years. Then Hinkle said, "After this meeting is over, you and I are going to have a very private little talk, Lieutenant, about your attitude towards women in service to our country, and about women in general, and about your future not only here at Roswell, but in the Air Force."

"Yes, sir. I didn't really mean anything disrespectful about Mrs. Gaines, sir."

"Save it for someone who doesn't know any better."

The door to the room opened on Celeste wearing the clichéd and stereotypical white lab coat with her blond hair pulled back into a tight bun at the back of her head. She looked older than her thirty-one years, and tired. As she steamed into the room, she said, "Gentlemen," without inflection and without looking at Walker.

"I thank you for coming today, Agent. Gaines" said Hinkle. "I know you have a busy schedule. I promise you that I am going to do everything in my power today to resolve the conflict between you and Lieutenant Walker that seems to be getting worse every day. You two have been at each other's throats for too long, and I intend for that to end after this meeting."

Celeste sat down and began to chew the fingernail of the first digit of her left hand. Her eyes never left Hinkle's face.

The commander continued, "Mrs. Gaines, please tell me in your own words how you see your problem with Lieutenant Walker and how you think it can best be resolved."

Celeste dropped her finger from her mouth.

"Lieutenant Walker has done nothing but interfere with possibly the single most important scientific investigation in all of recorded history, the study of a life-form alien to our planet. The philosophical implications alone are staggering. I don't know if he's interfering out of ignorance or stupidity, no disrespect intended, Lieutenant. And, frankly, I have no idea how this can be resolved other than by completely and permanently removing Mr. Walker from the project."

Toren's face went rigid.

Hinkle asked, "Lieutenant Walker? This seems to be a personality conflict to me. How do you think it can be resolved?"

"With all due respect, she ignores every rule and regulation on the base anytime she feels like it in the name of 'science', Commander Hinkle. And as the head of security for this top secret project, I simply cannot allow that. It jeopardizes not only her safety, but the integrity of the project. On top of that, she has made not one iota of progress in her 'investigation' of that thing in the tub."

Celeste fumed. "He has no concept or understanding of the scientific methods of discovery, Commander. It takes time, concentration, and dedication to unravel a mystery of this magnitude. My work is sometimes painfully slow. But every failure teaches me and my consultants as much as every success. I only ask that Lieutenant Walker do his job and keep… his…flat…nose…out of mine, uninterrupted."

Toren clenched his hands that were lying on the table. "She is a security risk, plain and simple. She comes and goes at all times of the day and night. She ignores all security check points. Half of the time, I don't even know what 'scientist' she is leading into the lab to observe that thing. On one occasion, she even forgot to seal the door to the lab behind her. She ignores military protocol and thinks she owns that thing which is actually the sole property of the American government."

"That thing that you and your men call 'The Blob', crossed millions of miles in a flying saucer so complex that we don't even know its source of propulsion yet. That thing is not a dog or a bug or a germ for you to step on. It is a sentient creature intelligent enough to not only build that saucer but to conquer space. I'm sorry to have to state the obvious, Base Wing Commander Hinkle. As for the military owning it, no government or agent of government, including the CIA can own a sentient being. I'm certain we outlawed slavery years ago. And if it takes us ten years, or twenty years, or twenty life times to finally break the code, so to speak, to communicate with him, to learn from it, then so be it."

"Him? Communicate with it, don't you mean? It doesn't even have a mouth!!"

"Thank you for the correction. It is true this creature appears to have no gender. Our working hypothesis is that it is not one creature, but a self-contained colony of tiny, symbiotic creatures living in a protective 'hard-water' skin, if you will, and able to communicate among themselves by something we might call telepathy."

There was a long moment of silence as Walker looked at Hinkle and shook his head in disbelief, and Hinkle seemed to look at nothing.

Sneering, Walker said, "And my working hypothesis is that the thing in the tub has become an obsession for a third rate scientist who is way in over her head in that gob of mucous but is trying to make a name for herself on the military's nickel."

"Which still puts me several steps above the knuckle-dragging troglodyte that I'm wasting precious time talking at, not to, right now."

"A high compliment coming from a self-important, ball-breaking, closet lesbian bi…"

Hinkle's fist stuck the top of the table.

He barked, "That's enough!!"

Both Celeste and Walker fell silent, looking at anything in the room except one another.

Hinkle waited several moments before speaking.

His tone was evenly modulated as he said, "This ends now.

"To begin, both of you are mistaken in your belief that you are somehow in charge of this project. Listen carefully. On this base, I am in charge of both of you. I am in charge of the alien creature in that tub. But even I am not the final authority over what we do or do not do during our investigation into that thing. That authority rests with people who shall remain nameless but who make you and me look like we're toddlers in kindergarten. Do you both understand that?" Celeste nodded her head. Walker said, "Yes, sir."

"Mrs. Gaines, you will continue to report directly to me."

Celeste said, "Gladly. So, then, who will Toren report to?"

"As for you, Lieutenant Walker, your position as head of security for this project is terminated…"

His face flushed red, Walker barked, "What…?!?" and half rose from his chair.

"Sit down, Lieutenant. As I said, you are no longer in charge of security for this project."You are excused, Mrs. Gaines."

"You are not excused, Mr. Walker."

Celeste pushed her chair back, rose from it, and walked to the door. She opened the door and glanced back over her shoulder.

If Walker could have spit blood from his eyes, he would have done so.

Celeste said, "Thank you, Commander Hinkle. See yah around, honey pie," winked at Toren, and closed the door behind her.

As the door closed, Hinkle said, "Because of your narrow-minded, boorish treatment of Mrs. Gaines, far below the behavior that is expected of an officer in the United State Air Force towards any woman, much less one in the service of our country, you will be reassigned to another job on base, Mr. Walker, to be determined by me at a later date."

Hinkle's raised hand, palm forward, stopped Walker from responding.

"I am not finished yet. It is only because you are so young, and because I see great potential in you, Lieutenant Walker, that I don't just kick your butt out of the Air Force right now, do you understand me?"

Toren said, "Yes, sir."

Hinkle pushed his chair back, rose, and walked to the door. He turned and looked back at Walker, sitting like a zombie at the table.

"Just sit there until you cool down, son. You will hear from me again, and soon, Lieutenant. Good day."

It was at that moment that the disdain, disgust, and sexual tension that Walker had felt for Celeste hardened and turned into a hatred that would only intensify with time.

CHAPTER EIGHT
MONDAY, JANUARY 13TH, 1948, 7:34 PM, ROSWELL AIR FORCE BASE, ROSWELL, NEW MEXICO

On Tuesday, January 14th, Agent Celeste Gaines mailed her report to the regional director of the CIA on the accidental death of Lucas Carn.

The entire report was a lie.

It wasn't an accident.

•••

Lucas Carn hated the blubbery red slab of alien mucous throbbing in the shallow, silver, concave tub in the center of the stainless steel room. As the civilian janitor stared at the horror through the small, heavy glass window in the thick, metal door to the room, he had no idea what it was, but it scared the living hell out of him.

He wasn't alone in his fear of the unknown. That was why the first goal of Celeste and the small band of military personnel who had arrived at the wreckage of the flying saucer had been secrecy. The first had made the second goal a frantic and intense struggle to evacuate the thing from the saucer alive. That had been very much like playing Russian roulette with all but one of the gun's chambers loaded.

Celeste hadn't had a clue whether the confusing chaos of tubes and wires that ran from the walls of the flying saucer to the body of that horror were life sustaining or not. They were all attached to seamless ports in the walls of the spacecraft. Of the few that were attached to the alien by a metallic band around the thing's middle, did one or more pump its own alien air into the monster? Was Earth's air poison to the alien? At the time, she had had no idea that the thing had no lungs. How did it breathe? And food? It had no mouth; how did it eat? Would a grain of rice slaughter it? When they got it out of the flying saucer, would the Earth's sun instantly burn the blob into a crisp, black, cow patty? If the tubing directly attached to the slimy blob was not a life support system, was it the means by which the flying saucer was navigated?

There were too many unknowns and no time for cautious experimentation. Celeste's heart had painfully skipped a beat or two as each tube had been cautiously detached from its port.

Lucas Carn's heart had also jumped as the janitor tapped the glass window in the metal door behind which the alien lay with a dirty fingernail. Then he pulled the double surgeon's mask pooled around his neck up over his mouth and nose.

It would do little to filter the thing's filthy alien germs, Lucas thought, but it was better than nothing.

His fifth grade education hadn't taught him that the box was an electronic lock. But Lucas punched in the numbered code on the little box next to the door with a heavily gloved finger as he had done dozens of times in the past.

The door slowly and laboriously swung open. Lucas pushed his janitor's cart filled with a dust mop and pan, a broom, wet wipes, towels, trash can liners, and a large trash can into the little metal room, waiting with a wary eye as the door swung closed behind him.

After the door had hissed shut, he opened the front of his protective overalls and removed a small, silver flask from his breast pocket. Lucas was in the habit of imbibing Kentucky bourbon to ease the mundane sameness of his job, and cleaning the stainless steel prison for a huge piece of crap deserved a larger than usual swig.

As he lowered the flask and wiped his mouth, Lucas had an epiphany that he knew would surely amuse his fellow janitors on the base during their break later that night. Grinning, he walked over to the slobber of alien life, and, raising his flask over the center of the pulsating ochre, let a slow drizzle of bourbon drip onto the alien.

He began to say, "Thisss one's fer you, shi…"

The alien blob exploded up in an eldritch wave.

Lucas looked up into the horror of its unhuman face and tried to scream. The flask fell from his hand, clattered on the metal floor, and lay still.

The alien horror fell and swallowed Lucas whole.

Lucas tried to scream again but his mouth and lungs were quickly filling with rancid, alien spume.

His final irrational thought as he franticly squirmed inside the revolting alien mucous and just before his brain exploded was regret over his decision.

He was really torn up over it.

WEDNESDAY, AUGUST 13TH, 1952, 9:34 PM, ROSWELL AIR FORCE BASE, ROSWELL, NEW MEXICO

Second Lieutenant Charles Wood asked, "When will I get the code?"

Lieutenant General Toren Walker glanced at Wood's square, brown Asian face and severely cropped brown hair, then punched numbered buttons on the punch pad next to the interior door of the service elevator as he grinned wanly.

He said, "'Impatience can cause wise people to do foolish things,' Lieutenant Wood. You'll get the code when I say you'll get it."

The elevator lurched and slowly began to sink from the basement of the airplane hangar to its secret subbasement with a metallic groan.

"I still don't understand all of the secrecy, sir," said Wood.

"It's not the job of a Second Lieutenant to understand anything, Mr. Wood. That's one of the reasons why you don't have the code. The only reasons that you are here at all are that you've won the confidence and trust of your superior officers, I'm getting a little older, and they're probably grooming you to replace me, and, mainly, because I need someone to carry my attaché case. Understand?"

"Oh, sir, I can't imagine…"

"Wood!" interrupted Walker. "One of the other reasons you are here is that you can't imagine. Now, you talk too much. Try listening and watching instead."

"Sir. Yes, sir."

The elevator lurched to a stop and its doors slid open on a dimly lit hallway that looked more like a tunnel made from huge metallic sections welded together. Without hesitation, Walker stepped out into the hall with the familiarity of long use as Wood followed, trying to absorb everything that he saw.

Without saying it, he noted that what he saw was nothing out of the unusual. The tunnel was about thirty yards long with a line of naked light bulbs embedded in its ceiling and strung down its center. Nothing was stored against its walls. It ended in a closed, windowless door with another punch pad in the wall next to its doorjamb.

When he and his Second Lieutenant reached the door, Toren Walker punched in another secret code and the door hissed back into a pocket in the wall. Toren grunted and stepped inside. Wood followed him.

The General turned back to the open doorway, punched more numbers into a punch pad on the interior wall of the room, and watched as the door slid closed with a sigh.

What Wood saw as Toren did so was something out of the unusual, at least some things beyond his experience.

A man in a dirty white lab coat stood in the middle of the room, watching both of them. He was middle-aged with thinning brown hair and wore protective eyewear pushed up to the hairline of his forehead, and a heavy pair of gloves. Almost every inch of every wall was covered with machinery and equipment beyond Wood's comprehension. In front of the man and on a long metal table stood an odd patchwork of metal struts. The cylinder was about four feet long and a foot in circumference and seemed to be made of long, silver, twisted strands of something like a huge stick of licorice.

Standing by Wood's side, Walker said, "Second Lieutenant Wood, meet Frank Abramson, one of the leading scientists in America and the head of the scientific arm of Project B.L.O.O.D.T.I.D.E. I can't even pronounce his official title.

"Frank, this is Second Lieutenant Charles Wood, my shadow for a time and a real dumb ass. You know why we are here, and you know me. So do for Wood what you do for me. Use small words.

"Have you finally found out anything new about that … thing?"

"Good to see you to, Toren," said the scientist and turned to focus on the object on his table. "I wish I could tell you that I've unraveled the mystery of what you call 'that thing', but I don't know much more than the last time we met, and not much more than when I started on this project, what, has it been five years?"

"Indeed it has, Frank."

"To bring your 'dumb ass' Asian friend up to speed, this object, and one other that was found in the wreckage of the flying saucer that crashed near here in '47, is not organic. It is not alive. We are certain of that. It is made of the same alien material as the flying saucer, but we have been unable to identity what it is by our periodic table of elements. It seems to have no seams or sections, one end is closed and the other has an opening that is about twelve centimeters deep. It resists x-rays, it can be scratched with a diamond, and that's about all that we know."

Lt. Wood swallowed hard. "A flying saucer…?!"

Toren said, "Just listen, kid. Remember? Of course you know, Frank, that if its secrets can be plumbed, it could add a great deal to our technology no matter what the thing might be."

It looked like Abramson was going to say, "Du-uh" but caught himself in time. Instead, he said, "Oh, no one understands that better than me, Lt. General Walker, sir. But I've tried every test I know, as have the handful of my fellow scientists that you've allowed down here, and will certainly continue to find answers. But the absolute truth is, as of this moment, that my little pet here could be anything from an alien weapon of immense power to a toilet seat."

Wood opened his mouth to speak but Walker's raised right hand stopped him. There was no discernible expression on his flat face.

"Not now, Wood. You'll know shortly.

"Well, Frank, I wish I could say it was a pleasure seeing you again, but it wasn't. Send my love to your wife and kids. I'll probably see you at the company picnic."

Toren began to turn back to the closed door when Frank added, "Sure thing, Lieutenant General Walker. I really am sorry, Toren. Really."

As he approached the door but without turning to face the scientist, Walker said, "I know. I know. Now, get back to work."

As the door to the lab slid closed behind him, Toren turned to Wood and found the completely bewildered expression he expected.

"Now, kid, what I'm going to tell you from this moment on will be repeated to no one, and I mean no one, forever. National Security and all of that bunk. Do you understand?

"C'mon," he added and began to walk down the hall.

Inside the lab, Abramson sighed and said, "Well, back to work."

He absentmindedly patted the top of the twist of silver licorice three times.

An incredibly intense, soundless, searing beam of light discharged out of its opening.

The wall facing it exploded with tornadic force, disintegrating into red hot dust and shards of glass and metal.

Abramson desperately tried to jerk his protective eyewear down with his right hand. But his face and that hand and his body were torn to ribbons, shrapnel instantly dismembering him, shredding Abramson like cheese, before his hand ever touched the glasses.

The lab's doorway was blown out and apart like tissue paper to scatter in little burning patches of metal and little pieces of Frank Abramson across the floor of the hall.

In the hallway, Toren and Wood were almost thrown off of their feet by the percussive blast and were deafened by the huge but muffled sound of the explosion in such a small, confined space.

Lt. General Toren Walker grabbed Lt. Charles Wood's bicep, and both men ran back down the hall towards the lab.

Both knew that Abramson would not play in the three legged race in the company picnic that year.

"THE WALL FACING IT EXPLODED..."

CHAPTER NINE
SUNDAY, SEPTEMBER 12TH, 1954, 8:15PM
ROSWELL AIR FORCE BASE, REBUILT RESEARCH LAB

He looked most like an ancient woodcut of the Norse God Thor.
His heavy, long red beard and hair, both unkempt, were in stark contrast to the stained gray jumpsuit that was the uniform he wore as a maintenance man on the base. The identification card he wore on a lanyard that fell to mid-chest announced his civilian status on a military base. A lidded, yellow, plastic tub serving as a trash can on the front of his metal cart and the assortment of cleaning products, paper and cloth towels, and plastic bottles of solvents stacked on the shelves on the back of the cart accurately completed the mundane, if somewhat inaccurate, stereotype of janitors throughout the civilized world. "Thor's" heavily lidded eyes implied that I.Q. was not his forte. In fact, he looked somewhat slovenly, uneducated, and as if he had never even heard the word forte.

As the janitor stood by the side of the cart, he punched numbered buttons on the punch pad next to a service elevator with a finger stained yellow from nicotine, and grinned rather brainlessly. There was an open pack of cigarettes in the breast pocket of his long-sleeved shirt. He was whistling to himself with a lisp.

He heard the elevator lurch and slowly begin to rise with a low, metallic growl from the recently rebuilt subbasement to the basement of the airfield hanger where he waited. Its door opened and he pushed his cart in and followed it. He punched in a number on a punch pad inside the elevator.

Thor watched the descending numbers above the closed elevator door blink on and off as the elevator sank. Neither he nor anyone else could have identified the name of the song he was whistling as it sank.

The elevator finally lurched to a stop and its door slid open on a dimly lit hallway that had once looked like a tunnel made from huge metallic sections welded together. After the accidental explosion that had destroyed the original tunnel and lab, the hall had been rebuilt as a rectangular passage. Without hesitation, Thor stepped out into the hall with the inattentive familiarity of long use, pushing his cart before him.

The tunnel was still about thirty yards long with a line of naked light bulbs hanging from its ceiling that ran down its center. Nothing was stored against the stark, metal walls. It ended in a closed, windowless door with another punch pad in the wall next to its doorjamb. A guard in a military uniform with a rifle strapped over one shoulder and across his chest stood next to the door. The guard did nothing to acknowledge the maintenance man's approach.

When the red-bearded man reached the guard and the door, the maintenance man tipped an imaginary cap out of respect. Saying nothing, the guard turned slightly and punched in four numbers on the pad. The janitor stepped forward and punched in an additional four numbers, and the door hissed back into a pocket in the wall. The guard returned to his half comatose state of mind and the janitor grunted and stepped inside. The door slid closed behind him with a sigh.

He immediately took a screwdriver from the left pants pocket of his jumpsuit and quickly stepped up to the light switch next to the door. He took off its cover and gently pulled out the wires beneath. Without hesitation, he disconnected the wires that turned on the hidden surveillance cameras around the room when the light switch was flipped up.

What Thor saw then was neither something out of the ordinary nor unexpected. He had seen it many times before.

Most of every wall was covered with complicated machinery and equipment. In front of him and on a metal table at about level with his knees stood an unusual patchwork of metal struts. The cylinders were about four feet long and a foot around and seemed to be made of long silver strands twisted into a huge stick of licorice.

Even though he knew it impossible, he looked around to see if anyone else was watching.

He took off the lid of the garbage can and set in against the side of the cart. Then, gingerly, he removed the alien weapon from its stand and placed it in the garbage can.

He removed his package of cigarettes with the matchbook stuffed in its cellophane covering, took one out, then removed and opened the matchbook. He tore out a match and struck it into fire, stuck the cigarette in his mouth, and lit it with the match.

He took his time to smoke the tobacco down to its filter, making sure the ashes fell into the garbage can. Then he crushed out what remained of the ember between his thumb and forefinger and dropped the butt in the garbage can.

Thor slowly repeated every step of preparing and smoking a second cigarette. Feeling he had fulfilled the needed time to fool the guard into thinking he'd done something to clean something in the room, he replaced the lid on the garbage can.

He wheeled his cart back to the light switch and reconnected the wires to the surveillance cameras. He replaced the cover. Then he rapped twice on the metal door. It slid open with a hiss.

The guard gave him no more attention when he wheeled the cart back down the corridor to the service elevator than when the janitor had first entered.

The elevator door slid open and Thor pushed the cart inside. He stepped in after it.

He watched the ascending numbers above the closed elevator door blink on and off as the elevator rose. The service elevator finally lurched to a stop and its door slid open.

Thor left the elevator and wheeled his cart down a hallway to an exit opening onto an alley behind the airplane hangar. He opened that door.

A large van was waiting for him, its engine idling, and its back doors open.

The janitor took the alien weapon out of the trash can, put it in the back of the van, and closed the vans doors. He pushed the cart and all of its contents to one side of the alley.

He opened the passenger side door of the van and slid inside on a bench seat.

The man behind the steering wheel threw the van into gear. It began to pull out of the alley as Thor stripped off his red mustache and his unruly red beard and let them fall to the floor.

He sighed deeply, and said, "Damn."

He had no idea he had opened Pandora's Box.

CHAPTER TEN
THURSDAY, FEBRUARY 9TH, 1967, 8:46PM, ROSWELL AIR FORCE BASE, ROSWELL, NEW MEXICO

Celeste's eyes were swollen and red. Her exhaustion was evident by the half moons of sweat staining the underarms of her lab coat, in the slump of her shoulders, and the sluggishness of her steps. Her legs felt like they were full of lead, and her breathing was somewhat shallow and was the only sound except for the filtered air being circulated through the room by vents in the metal walls.

She looked at the alien placenta, the Blob lying in the concave chair that had been salvaged from the wreckage of its flying saucer almost twenty years ago, immovable except for the red maggots forever writhing inside its hard-water shell. The alien's chair stood in the middle of the hermitically sealed, sterilized laboratory buried deep beneath a building on the airfield above; it looked like the inside of a thermos except for one large, plate glass window, triple-paned, behind which most of Celeste's experiments on the alien were conducted.

Next to the pilot's seat stood a small, metal cart on wheels. On that cart was a metal tray, and on that tray were the items to which the alien had been exposed that day. There was a small, leafless branch from a scrub oak, a dead lizard, a strip of aluminum foil, and an open container of tap water. The alien had not negatively or positively reacted to any of them. As was indicated on the paper in her clip-board, these items were numbered 1,237, 1,238, 1,239, and 1,240.

The only thing that Celeste and her team had learned in the last twenty years had been learned when the alien had been hastily removed from the wreckage of the flying saucer. It had not died from exposure to the atmosphere of Earth. It had not died from exposure from any of the germs contacted, and, in turn, its alien 'germs,' if any, had not killed anyone involved in its removal.

Everything else thought about the alien being was pure conjecture. And the patience of the few scientists involved, of the military hiding and protecting the project, and of the governmental bean-counters off base, was wearing thin, and Celeste knew it.

She tapped her ball point pen on the sheet of paper on the metal clip-board covered with her notes, and sighed deeply.

Absent-mindedly, she attempted to stick the pen in the left pocket of her slacks, but missed the opening. The pen fell to the floor and rolled several feet in front of her without her noticing the sound.

Celeste closed the cover of the metal clip-board in her hands in disgust. She took several steps towards the only door to the lab that could only be opened by a code tapped into a punch pad on the wall by it.

She stepped on the ball point pen; her leg shot out from under her.

Celeste threw out her left hand to stop her fall.

It landed into the side of the K'huprician.

An electric shock, an intense thrill, ran up her arm into her shoulder, throwing her head back. She dropped the clip board. Her eyes rolled back in her head as her mind exploded in a confetti of multi-colored lights.

Her body spasmed. She staggered, but did not fall.

She almost swallowed her tongue. Her pupils dilated.

Gasping for breath and inexplicably floating in nothingness, Celeste lowered her head and suddenly, impossibly, irrationally saw a pale green sky thousands of feet below her, an unending alien desert beneath the sky, and three enormous, blood-red suns low on the horizon. The greatest of the three suns was the size of size of her thumb.

Twilight was fast approaching, but, despite that, the blistering, life-threatening heat made her feel her blood was boiling in her veins.

As far as she could see, huge fields of a brownish mold as fragile as peanut brittle formed random splotches on a desert that was also pockmarked with enormous craters and randomly covered with worm-like mounds. Although these startling images were completely alien to her, Celeste knew this was the Blob's planet. This was K'hupric. And she knew it was a parched, desolate planet that crawled underground with a dying race of squirming amorphous bags of mucous moving sluggishly through an endless web of tunnels.

They were the community, the One of the thing on her table. Sslits.

Disembodied and overcome with curiosity, Celeste slowly sank lower and lower and lower to its pimpled surface. She knew these putrid horrors were called Hive, and that she was floating above a planet that was no more than a blister on the universe, a jigsaw puzzle of cracked earth.

Floating a dozen feet above the surface of the planet, Celeste paused in her descent to study one of the massive mounds of yellow sand, an alien ant hill taller than any other object within her sight on the otherwise deserted, exhausted desert. Above the mound, the pale green air shimmered from the heat.

And as she watched, four indeterminate things slowly rose up from a hidden or camouflaged exit, a wormhole, to the relatively flat top of the mound. At first, they looked like gigantic turtles. But it took only a second for Celeste to realize that each of the red bags of maggots wore a ridged carapace over its back that looked like a turtle's shell.

And she knew that one of these unhumans was the alien now lying, seemingly comatose, on the concave chair next to Celeste, frozen in place by the horrendous vision violating her mind.

Each of the aliens at one of the corners of what looked somewhat like a sled was pushing it along the surface until it reached the center of the mound. It left a wide furrow behind it in the sand. On that sled was an alien slug, a member of the things called Sslits, and she knew that she was witnessing a ritual for one of their dead.

When the sled was in place, a long, thin tube, a proboscis, snaked out from each of the monstrous creatures and attached itself to the corpse. And as she watched in horror, each of the four aliens began to suck the dead corpse dry, not because they were cannibalistic, but because each liquid drop was utterly priceless because water was life and almost none existed on K'hupric outside of what was treasured and stored in each gelatinous body of each K'huprician.

Celeste said, "No, no, no, no" and jerked her left hand out of the Blob.

She looked down at the thin, red slime that covered that hand.

She gasped, grabbing her throat with her right hand.

She fell to the floor of the lab, unconscious.

Several days later, she burned the film from the surveillance cameras in a trash can.

CHAPTER ELEVEN
NOVEMBER 15, 1996, 9:30AM, EASTWOOD MALL, TULSA, OKLAHOMA.

Speaking into the hidden microphone in the lapel of her coat, Celeste Gaines said, "Sslits. Follow me."

But Sslits stood motionless, terrified. The alien was dressed in a bulky, beige overcoat, huge, black, construction worker's steel-toed boots, and an equally oversized slouch hat as it stood in the ebb and flow of human flesh that washed around it in the shopping mall. Celeste could not tell if a creature that could not conceive of singularity was nevertheless frozen with fear by the crowd of living creatures moiling about—theoretically like the hive it came from on its planet—or if its struggle to maintain a vaguely humanoid shape was a terrific effort that required its entire focus.

Today was a huge gamble for Celeste, but the earlier trials designed by her to acclimate Sslits to society at much smaller venues had worked over the long years of trial and error. Those years had taken an emotional toll on her. She was psychologically numb and it had come to the point that she almost didn't really care whether she succeeded or failed anymore.

She was an enigma to herself and her associates now, eighty years old but looking as young as she had in 1947; looking even younger than she had on Friday, December 31st, 1971 when she had first accidently 'entered' the alien for the first time when she was fifty-five years old. She still looked like the blond, blue-eyed, comely but not beautiful girl of average height and weight and figure that had made her the American ideal of the girl next door when she as a teenager. Her eighty years had also brought with it much indifference, some wisdom, and the patience of Job, but, impossibly, no permanent change in her face or body. Her life, however, had been a living hell, a nightmarish absurdity.

She didn't even care that the meager crowd was peppered with NIAR agents, and probably a half-a-dozen spies from countries like Russia, England, Iran, and France. They were a constant now, and had been par for the course of her life for at least the last five years.

Speaking into the hidden microphone, Celeste repeated, "Sslits. Follow me."

The K'huprician still did not move. The sparse crowd of shoppers around him seemed oblivious to the alien. That and the fact that Sslits had walked under his own will into the mall meant that her experiment was at least a partial success. That it wouldn't move now was a total mystery like most of what the alien did or did not do in response to her commands.

Since 1947, the thing had destroyed her marriage, was the reason she had lost custody of her two children to her husband, and had made her a laughing stock in the scientific community. She had become the target of half of the clandestine agencies in the world and the butt of nasty little jokes told around half of the water coolers in the offices in America.

So what difference did it really make she thought *to be standing in the middle of a mall in Tulsa next to an alien from another world dressed like Humphrey Bogart in a Sam Spade movie?*

Celeste knew it just wasn't going to be her day. The incompatible smells of pretzels, friend chicken, giant cookies, and Chinese and Greek cuisine from the food court was a bit unpleasant. The garish signs and shop fronts full of a chaos of faddish clothing, shoes, recorded music, posters, books, greeting cards and so much more were not to her taste as well. And the instrumental versions of Rock and Roll songs that had been popular twenty years ago that played from hidden speakers under the low murmur and occasional laughter from the shoppers just added to her frustration.

She was too busy thinking of the only alien on earth whose pseudo-face at the moment looked like Billy Graham, the television evangelist, with an exaggerated and razor sharp jaw. *We should have never let it get addicted to television* she thought. *Or radio. Or muscle-man magazines.*

Into her coat's lapel, and for the third time, she said, "Sslits, follow. Now"

Sslits did nothing.

It had been forty-nine years ago that the tiny scientific team of experts had been assigned to thoroughly study the extraterrestrial. Celeste and Toren Walker had been founding members. And it had taken decades of her life and the lives of countless others, the deaths of three men, and lost arms and fingers and faces, to admit what was obvious from the moment of first discovery of the wreckage, that the thing in the flying saucer was utterly unhuman.

Unhuman.

Over the years, other words describing the extraterrestrial in the shallow, silver tub would be added; unpredictable, incomprehensible, unnatural, uncanny, vicious, and obsessive. It had also proven to possess only one human emotion or instinct: survival.

It was unhuman.

The scientists and military personal that had secretly drizzled into and out of the base at Roswell in a steady stream had initially learned much more about the living blob than from the bodies of three of the alien crew that had died in the crash. Their corpses had looked like broken glass jars of jelly smeared over the silver walls of the spacecraft. From those bodies, the team had discovered that two long held theories—that water and some form of oxygen are fundamental for life to exist—were true. Sslits was mostly a liquid similar to water, although the percentage seemed to change by the second, and the alien was able to breathe Earth's atmosphere. They had also postulated that the lack of any recognizable internal organs, including a brain, meant that the functions of such organs were performed on a cellular level, i.e., "the squirming maggots." Its entire body was its brain, its liver, its kidneys, its lungs.

Eventually, the B.L.O.O.D.T.I.D.E. team would also learn that Sslits was incredibly adaptable to any environment or situation. That plus its travel across space indicated an advanced but impenetrable intelligence.

The ship and everything else associated with the slimy, giant amoeba were made of no known element on Earth.

It seemed to Celeste that death and dismemberment were quite a price to pay so that the blob from outer space could stand in the center of a shopping mall with her with most of the human face it had sculpted obscured by a Fedora.

Again, Celeste said, "Sslits. Follow me," but Sslits did not move.

Until 1958, Celeste had called it "the Blob," until the silly Science-Fiction movie that was a surprising hit at drive-in theaters came along. Sslits is what the thing found in the flying saucer had begun calling itself after fifteen years of incomprehensive gurgles, sloshes, and blurbles.

Her anger and frustration growing, Celeste barked, "Sslits, move!"

The team also eventually learned that its K'huprician scout ship had been driven to ground by a cracked widget...and by madness. A word that sounded like K'hupric was what it called the universe or planet, they were sure, from which it had traveled. The enormity of the Atlantic was an obscenity of excess. Celeste's team had also posited that the sight of so much water in the Pacific was more than they could bear and had driven the flying saucer's crew to the brink of madness. On their arid, blistered world, water was rare; water was life...and death.

Sslits stood motionless.

Celeste glanced around the few people shopping in the mall to see if they had drawn attention to themselves. They had not.

In a sense, it wasn't a surprise to Celeste that Sslits often did not respond to her. For more than fifteen years, even the world's foremost linguists had failed to communicate with this sole surviving alien from the Roswell crash. Sslits couldn't tell the team its name, though, or anything else—until someone accidentally dropped a transistor radio into its liquid head in September of '62, thereafter enabling it to somehow grow itself a 'throat'.

Subsequently, the B.L.O.O.D.T.I.D.E. team had been almost driven mad by the K'huprician singing the song "Sherry" by the rock 'n roll group, *The Four Seasons*, two hundred and seventy three times in a row. Yes, they had counted.

No one knew how or why the accident had happened, no one except Celeste who had done it but kept her clumsiness a secret. Celeste had grown to hate that song, but it turned out that repetition was and is essential to a creature of collective consciousness whose world is one big, bloody bee hive. And, since it couldn't think independently...

On Earth Seven, Celeste became Sslits' hive.

She offered a silent prayer to the God whose existence she doubted that those hidden speakers wouldn't play an instrumental version of *Sherry*, before she said, "Sslits. Follow me!!!" and The Blob finally took a clumsy step forward and stopped. The sounds of the mall had obscured the slosh of its footfall from the shoppers around it.

At the same moment, on the second above-ground tier of the mall—overhead and slightly on Celeste's right side—only a handful of shoppers heard a young ebony haired woman named Lisa Ferry yelling at an athletic young man, and saw her punching his chest with a finger. The couple was standing five feet in front of one of the large, tempered glass panels framed with metal supporting rods that rose about above her and served as protective guard rails.

"Stay away from me!" she barked from the beautiful, smooth, brown face of an East Indian woman now twisted by fear and anger. "I'm not going to tell you again, it's over! Stop following me!!"

She poked his chest again with a finger.

"If you don't leave me alone, I'll call the police!!"

With a nasty grin, he said, "Yeah? What you gonna call 'em, Lisa?" and lunged forward, his arms rigid and his palms forward, and, hitting her on her collarbone, pushed her back.

She staggered back two steps, surprised.

The few shoppers near them who noticed instinctively stepped back.

Her anger escalating, she shouted, "I mean it, you jerk!!"

"Then call them! I'll give you the damn dime!"

So saying, Lisa's tousle-headed lover lunged forward, his arms rigid and his palms forward, and pushed her harder.

Lisa staggered back another two steps.

One of the shoppers nearby yelled, "Stop him!!" but did nothing.

Another shopper whispered to her companion, "Get security!!"

Lisa's voice shook as she whispered, "Brad...?!

Brad pushed her again with terrific force.

She staggered back and the glass panel shattered behind her.

Instantly snatching her left leg under her thigh with his left hand, Brad jerked up and, with all of his strength, pushed against her chest with his right hand as he lifted her up by her thigh and threw her over the outwardly exploding glass wall.

Following the sound of breaking glass, Celeste looked up from the floor of the mall. A small boy in a t-shirt, an old man in a baseball cap, and a child clutching his mother's waist also looked up, the child pointing with a finger on his pudgy free hand. A young woman carrying a sack among the shoppers screamed.

Lisa fell backwards in a shower of razor sharp glass shards, screaming and clutching at the air as she fell.

Watching Lisa fall, Celeste jerked the lapel of her overcoat up to her mouth and barked, "Sslits! Above!!"

Sslits looked up with faux eyes without pupils.

One woman in a now sea of upturned faces on the floor of the mall covered her mouth.

Sslits blinked its blank eyes.

The mother shook her child free of her waist, turned, and fled down the mall. The child cried as he watched his mother disappear down the plaza.

"CATCH!!" Celeste screamed inside the tiny microphone in her lapel that screamed inside Sslits' head.

The K'huprician tore off the Fedora. A long, red shock of something like spiked hair sprang up and back from where most humans had eyebrows to end the nape of its red neck. Its 'hair' looked like wheat blown in a violent wind; its face looked like a deeply concerned Billy Graham.

The alien's heavy boots fell sideways from its toeless feet.

Sslits tore open the overcoat, baring a massive red chest, and let the coat fall on the checkerboard floor.

Lisa was screaming her shriek diminishing as she fell.

Celeste hissed, "Sslits! Don't...kill...these," saying these because the alien could not conceive of singularity and therefore of words like her or this one or that woman.

In an instant, in the time it takes to inhale, Sslits' two massive legs merged into one, the alien dropped its enormously muscled arms to its sides, and exploded up like a powerful waterspout, gushing up its chest expanding, doubling in size as it rose, gushed up five, ten, then fifteen feet, its back arching as it rose until...

The girl impacted with Sslits!

Lisa Ferry fell backwards into the thick, jelly mucous of its grotesquely extended chest.

Then the barely conscious woman, her face still frozen in fear, slowly sank like molasses into the alien as Sslits also shrank its extended, merged leg back down to the floor. She sank deep into and then through Sslits, trailing spittles of slime as she fell out of the thing with a great sucking sound and harmlessly hit the floor under the monster.

Before her body had even struck the floor, Sslits was self-healing the ruptures in its body.

Most of the shoppers closest to Sslits receded like waves from a beach, then turned, almost as one, and fled, screaming and stumbling against and over one another, parting around and then reforming in back of four unmoving human piers in the mail that were spies.

As Celeste trotted the short distance to Sslits and the woman on the floor at its feet, she saw that one of the four human piers was Toren Walker, a tiny smile on his flat, furrowed face, sixty-five years old but still instantly recognizable as her former partner at the NIAR. She glanced back at Sslits, the minor rends in its body now mostly sealed, staring down at the woman on the floor at its reformed two toeless feet.

She glanced down at Lisa whose short gasps made her think of childbirth.

Lisa lay before Sslits, her eyelids closed over black pupils, her ebony hair a matted mess of red goo, and one of her legs elevated at a forty-five degree angle with its foot still immersed in the alien's back until it turned to face her. Sslits' chest was already reforming as the alien's body soundlessly sucked up the large, thin pool of liquid at its pseudo feet that had splattered out of it upon Lisa's impact. As Sslits continued to remold its faux-human shape, it looked down, emotionless, at Lisa.

Then the alien knelt, oozed both of its still oversized arms gently under the unconscious woman, and gently lifted her in its arms.

The alien rose, holding her against its massive chest.

Someone in the group of shoppers who had not run away began to clap nervously.

Sslits stood.

Several of those who had initially fled a short distance away rejoined the stunned group of shoppers and joined in the spattering of applause, consternation and fear mixed on their faces.

A little boy said, "Hey!!" with something of both fear and awe.

Waving her arms, Celeste ordered the shoppers nearest them to, "Please step back; step back, please. This is all part of a stunt for a movie. Everything is in control."

Lisa awoke in Sslits' arms even as the alien began to suck back into its six feet, five inch height.

Arching her back and with tears in her eyes, Lisa threw her arms around the alien's 'neck' and kissed Sslits' 'cheek.'

Sslits showed no visible response to her kiss as it gently lowered her to her feet.

Mixing with the applause, a few people in the crowd began to cheer.

Sslits touched its mouth with a faux hand.

Celeste said, "Oh, boy," and bit the fingernail of a digit of her left hand. "What the hell does that mean?"

Then she began to search the faces of the shoppers, searching for Toren Walker.

The three spies and Walker had disappeared as had many of the shoppers.

Celeste signed and said only to Sslits and herself, "Now how do I get you out of here?"

The K'huprician burbled, *Walk Like a Man.*

CHAPTER TWELVE

Former C.I.A. agent Celeste Gaines hadn't been as surprised by anything that day as much as she was by the appearance of former Air Force officer Toren Walker.

She had snarled, "Toren," under her breath as she had hustled the massive alien, still in his slouch hat and overcoat, into the double back doors of the large white van waiting outside the mall for them. Her lawyer, Larry Odom, who had been waiting behind its steering wheel, had seen the confusion and anger in her face, and had asked, "What?" as he thought, *now what the hell had she done this time.*

"Toren was inside," she said as she slammed one of the sliding doors closed. She stomped around the side of the van, wrenched the passenger door open, and slid towards Odom on the bench seat. She reached back and slammed the door closed.

"Hit it," she said.

Odom hit the gas pedal.

As the van picked up speed, she groused, "Toren damn Walker, Larry. I can't believe it? What do you know about this, huh? Have you been up to more of your old shenanigans again? Playing double agent?"

Odom stuck a Camel cigarette that he held habitually between the index and third fingers of his right hand into his mouth and inhaled.

"Well, C," Larry's nickname for her, "I don't know anymore about it than you, but I can't say I'm surprised."

He exhaled.

"I didn't say I was surprised, either, Larry" she lied. "I just want to know how the hell he knew we'd be in the mall today. You and I were supposed to be the only human beings above ground who knew."

She had refused to look at Larry Odom. Everything about his youth; his thick, black hair and eyebrows, his baby-smooth skin, his clear, blue eyes, his perfect nose and mouth, was off-putting to her. Well, maybe his mouth was a little too small for his face. That was not surprising since Larry was wrinkle-free, forty years younger than she and looked every day of it.

His black suit, white shirt, and tie with thin, diagonal, red lines had not been surprising either. He had worn that combination almost every day of his life. She thought he dressed more like a mortician than one of the highest paid lawyers in America.

Nothing surprised Celeste anymore.

Odom was pushing the van hard to put as much distance between themselves and the mall in as short a time as possible.

Celeste's mind raced with the van. Uncharacteristic of her, she decided to talk.

"I hadn't been surprised, Larry, when the National Institute for Alien Research was created as a special division of the military to oversee the protection, preservation, and exploitation of my alien monstrosity. Nor did it surprise me when the NIAR eventually replaced the transistor radio that had 'accidently' fallen into Sslits with a micro-transmitter and receiver, either. And, over the years, it was disgusting but I hadn't been surprised that the song *Sherry* that Sslits first heard on the radio was replaced by Madonna's *Like a Virgin*. Ultimately, what difference doesn't that make to me?

"Otherwise, communicating with a non-linear alien who would just as soon slaughter you as sing the latest noise passing for music was still as difficult on that first day as finding teats on a hog."

Odom said, "What has that got to do with anything?"

Celeste said, "I'm just thinking out loud, Larry. But I wouldn't expect you to understand that. Since when did any man ever communicate with a woman?"

Without taking his eyes off of the road, Odom said, "Well, at least you recognize I'm a man for a change."

Ignoring him in fear of losing her train of thought, Celeste continued, "Especially when the 'man' is an asexual alien...and the woman is an eighty-year-old divorcee, one who couldn't even remember why she originally code-named the project and the thing B.L.O.O.D.T.I.D.E. in 1957."

Odom said, "An ineffective acronym for Biological Liaison of Overarching Technologies Investigating Deciduous Extraterrestrials."

But Odom's words fell on deaf ears as Celeste descended into her own thoughts.

She was Celeste Gaines, ex-NIAR operative and, according to the covers of all the grocery store tabloids; Sslits was the alien she'd been sleeping with for more than a decade.

She was the Celeste, the woman who had filed the largest human rights case in American history on Feb. 4, 1973, when she was fifty-seven years old. Toren Walker's National Institute for Alien Research claimed they owned Sslits. She claimed otherwise.

Celeste had won the lawsuit in March of 1996 because of the ingenious but irritating man behind the steering wheel. She was too busy being unemployed to know how right she really was at the time. No one can own someone else.

Even if they deserve to.

The price for being right had been three million dollars in legal fees that Celeste didn't have, a pseudo-government agency shadowing her every move that refused to settle for anything less, another pending trial...

And now Toren Walker of the broad, somewhat flat face was back.

The only payback for Celeste in all of this was...

"At least Walker looks every bit as old as he really is!"

She had said it to no one in particular.

Odom nodded in the affirmative without looking at her.

As she had said it she thought of the applauding crowd in the mall only moments earlier and of the then fully conscious Lisa Ferry lovingly looking up into the empty eyes of an alien from another planet.

"Damn, Larry," she said. "Out of the frying pan into the fire.

"I've done it again, haven't I?"

CHAPTER THIRTEEN

TRIBUNE NEWSPAPER BUILDING, BRADY WAREHOUSE DISTRICT, TULSA, OKLAHOMA FRIDAY, NOV. 15TH, 1996

Celeste knew the knock on the door to her ramshackle room on the first floor of the long abandoned *Tulsa Tribune* newspaper building meant that her lawyer, Larry Odom, had arrived. After all, he was supposedly the only person outside of the landlord who knew that she and Sslits where holed up in the six story, red brick building across the railroad tracks that ran across the north side of downtown Tulsa.

She was still feeling the burn of having to pay the landlord more for a week of his silence than she paid her high priced lawyer in a year, especially since the building had no electricity or working bathroom. She had had to make do with camping equipment: four heavy-duty air mattresses staked two deep and two abreast for Sslits, a sleeping bag for herself, two pieces of luggage for her clothing, several propane lanterns, a compost toilet, and an ice chest.

Without looking up from *The Global Star*, the grocery store tabloid that she was reading, she said, "It's open."

In big, black letters, the headline on the front cover of the tabloid read:

SCIENTIST
SLEEPS WITH
ALIEN

Below was a drawing of a bulbous headed alien with huge eyes, one of the hundreds of published and broadcast variations of the little faux sketch she had done of Sslits and widely distributed in 1947 to misdirect the public from the truth. The irony had not escaped Gaines.

In smaller type, the headline on the back cover read:

" ...SHE SAW A DISGRUNTLED ODOM... "

Alien Is
Running for
President

The door swung open and she saw a disgruntled Odom standing in the doorway in the meticulously creased suit and tie, the shined shoes, and little briefcase in his left hand that were his trademarks. A Camel cigarette hung from his lower lip.

She said, "Oh, it's just you. Come in, Larry."

Celeste wore a fluffy, white robe and sat on a dilapidated folding chair that was the twin of another in an otherwise almost empty room. The microphone that she usually wore at her wrist was now pinned to the lapel of the robe.

She didn't know the history behind it, but she sat in a room that had once been the office of the entertainment editor of one of Tulsa's newspapers, the *Tulsa Tribune*.

Odom said, "Well, *that* is stupid beyond belief, Mrs. C. Anyone could have been on the other side of this damn door."

From behind the tabloid, she said, "Miss C, to you, sir. Nice to see you too, Larry. As I said, come in and don't let the damn door hit you in the butt when you do. There's another folding chair over there. Plant yourself in it."

As Odom looked around for the place to plant it, he said, "I swear to God, sometimes I think you're as thick as a brick."

He sat down in the other ratty folding chair facing hers, and placed his briefcase carefully on the floor by his left side. He took the cigarette out of his mouth.

"Before you say another word, Odom, tell me how Toren Walker knew we would be at the mall today, and why he was there. And don't pretend you don't know."

"Not a clue, but at least it wasn't the clown who replaced him. What's his name?"

"Charles Wood, Larry. Wood. He's just as big a rat as Walker."

Now smiling, Odom answered, "That's it. Charles Wood. What a pain in the butt."

Celeste slowly lowered the tabloid. Her expression was not welcoming. Odom's smile vanished and he averted his eyes.

What he had glimpsed were the heavy creases of parchment skin and a sallow face, heavy folds of flesh above slitted eyes, pencil-thin lips, a wrinkled forehead, and the yellowed hair like straw of an eighty year old woman.

Celeste folded the tabloid and laid it in her lap.

"Really, Odom. Really? Are you really that thin skinned, buckaroo? It's not like you haven't seen this before."

Still looking at anything in the room but Celeste, he said, "I know, I know. But the duration of, well, er, your youthfulness seems to be getting more and more brief."

Celeste ignored the statement and sighed. "It is what it is, you know. It's not something I have any control over. You stashed the van?"

"Yes. Yes, I did. I must admit," continued the lawyer, "that was a nice catch at the mall this morning. Do you remember that he can't kill again? The only thing that saved us last time is what saved our butts in the NIAR suit."

"I was sorta counting on that," said Celeste. "And he isn't a he and, in case you didn't notice, Sslits didn't kill again. In fact, the alien saved a life this time. Go figure.

"See if you can force yourself to look at me, honey. I know you can do it."

Odom looked at her.

"I wouldn't count on it—the suit—saving my favorite Martian much longer," Odom continued. "The court is eventually going to decide if Sslits is a sentient being and subject to our laws. By the way, it would help if I knew the answer for certain."

"I know, Larry. I know," Celeste said. "And, believe me do, I do appreciate everything you and your lawyer buddies have done to save my butt up to now."

She jerked a thumb to her right and over her shoulder to draw Odom's attention to the only other door in the room, one separating a second room from where they sat.

"You've done a great job of legally confusing that issue.

"Sslits is in what is pretending to be the bedroom, sitting alone on the mattresses in what I call his 'hibernation mode,' for lack of a better term, on the floor in there. I sure could have used your help to get the plastic slipcover on the mattresses, but that's water under the bridge.

"I wonder how 'he' sleeps. Sslits, I mean. Under any conditions. I know I don't."

Odom continued, "If the alien is ruled a 'man', then the NIAR has no legal ownership of it. But, then, if an incident like tonight had turned sour, that could leave Sslits open to manslaughter charges. It didn't, but the alien could have killed the woman who fell instead of saving her butt, and no one knows that better than you. That's why I'm telling you...no more of this superhero stuff."

Larry reached down, picked up his briefcase, and stood up from his chair.

"Worse yet, if it's ruled he's an animal..."

Celeste cut his thought short. "I know, I know. You don't have to say it again, Larry. I'm not stupid or deaf or mentally handicapped."

"I'm your lawyer, Celeste. You pay me to say it. Well, you'll pay me someday to say it."

Odom paused to add to the weight of his coming words.

"He'll be destroyed. I mean, it will be destroyed."

Larry walked to the door, but paused. He turned back to face Celeste again.

"This isn't exactly an isolated incident, Celeste. This has been going on for years to varying degrees. There's a big movement afoot at my law firm to drop you as a client."

"Little ol' me, Larry? Really? I didn't know movements had a foot."

"This is no laughing matter, Miss C. I will advise you again to drop what you have planned as your next little experiment to acclimate that thing you call Sslits into society. My partners are dead serious about washing their hands of you right now."

"I know you'll stop them from dropping me, Larry. After all, you're in love with me, sweetie. You can't keep your eyes off of me. We both know it, even though you try your best to hide it."

"You're full of crap, Celeste. Full of it."

Odom opened the door.

"By the way, I hope you don't mind my saying so...but you look like warmed-over death. You'd better get in there and let Frankenstein give you another sponge bath, honey."

"Why Frankenstein, Larry? Why not you, sweet cheeks?"

Odom's pasty face blushed.

"No. Well, you can at least take some consolation that your check's in the mail, which, to a lawyer, is better than sex."

As the door swung shut on Odom, Celeste added, "Next time, buttercup, I'll even put a stamp on the envelope."

The former CIA agent rose from her chair, weary and sore. She moaned as the arthritic pain ran through both of her knees and her left arm.

She said to herself, "Now don't you cry, honey. Maybe next time, he'll take the bait."

CHAPTER FOURTEEN

At that moment but miles away at the *Route 66 Motel* on 11th Street in Tulsa, Lisa Ferry was putting on her face in front of a mirror over her motel room's chest-of-drawers, thinking about her upcoming date with a moon man. She knew why it was so important that she succeed, and she knew how she would make it happen.

It was why she had followed the white van to the Tribune newspaper building in a taxi.

Everything had fallen literally into place. And although he didn't seem to understand half of what Lisa said in the brief moment that they had had together at Eastwood Mall, he understood kisses. Just like a real earth angel.

That much was obvious.

•••

Celeste bit the fingernail of a digit of her left hand. The reflection of her eighty year old heart-shaped face in the cheap mirror she held in her hand while she was sitting in her 'bedroom' was marked with an overwhelming weariness and sadness. She pursed her lips and raised a lipstick with a trembling left hand to her mouth. She dropped her hand with the lipstick in utter regret and resignation.

"I put you before my family," she said to the mirror. Her voice trembled. "My husband... even my children."

Her puffy eyes welled up with tears.

"You've cost me almost everything," Celeste whispered. "And why? Why have I done this? Out of a misplaced respect for all life?"

A tear began to run down her left cheek. She raised her wrinkled, liver-spotted right hand to wipe it away. Seeing her eight decades old hand reflected in the mirror, she let it drop.

"Why am I doing this?" Celeste asked of the otherwise silent room. "You can't even understand half of what I say."

Massive, its pseudo-human face still mimicking Billy Graham's face, its long, colorless shock of spiked hair swept back on its head by an invisible wind, Sslits stepped up and to the right side behind Celeste to join her reflection in the mirror.

The K'huprician gently placed its left hand on her left shoulder.

"And at the mall.' Celeste continued. "What the hell was that about? I haven't seen you experience a human emotion in forty-seven years. Why now?"

Hive die…again, the alien hissed.

Celeste turned her head and looked up at the alien's face. The whisper of a smile was on her wrinkled lips. She let the mirror in her hand slide from it to fall on the floor.

"What in the hell does that mean?" she asked, and placed her right hand over the back of Sslits' huge left hand. "Do you mean you couldn't let another 'hive' like me die again, even a human one? Do you mean something would…I don't know what you mean. Again.

"The 'hive like me' at the big buildings today, Sslits—the hive called Lisa whispered something to Sslits afterwards. What?"

Can you come out tonight? Sslits gurgled.

Placing its right hand on her right shoulder and letting its left hand fall to her left bicep, Sslits effortlessly lifted Celeste off of the chair.

Celeste said nothing as she let her head fall towards its chest.

As one they turned to face the four air mattresses, two stacked on top of two, on the floor that was set against one wall of the nondescript room. There was a propane lamp on the right side and the left side of the mattresses sitting on the bare, wooden floor. There was no decoration of any kind on the walls. There was only one window.

Sslits' huge overcoat, construction workers steel-toed boots, and an equally oversized slouch hat lay in a rumpled mess on the floor next to the left side of the mound of mattresses.

There was no vanity mirror behind them to reflect the backs of an old woman in a white robe and the hideous red alien.

•••

As Larry Odom walked down the hallway leading to the main entrance of the abandoned building, his mind wandered to the alien's makeshift bedroom…to what he knew was probably happening at that very moment.

To the perversion of human flesh and alien flesh entwined.

Of a phoenix rising from the ashes of death.

He stopped at the door, smoothed his hair down with his right hand, and then turned the doorknob. As he did so, he thought *Wet. Glistening with life. Reborn. Rejuvenated. New. Made young again in mind and body by her alien consort. Just as she had done over and over and over again through the years, allowing Sslits' alienness inside her in exchange for her restored youth. Temporary immortality. Temporary immorality.*

Odom shuddered at the very thought of what was happening to Mrs. C.

He stepped into the doorway of the main entrance and paused.

He made a mental note to himself to remember that phrase—temporary immortality—the next time he phoned in a little tidbit about the alien to the *Global Star* tabloid.

It was a dirty business, but Celeste needed the money.

•••

The room was full of flickering shadows and soundless except for Celeste's shallow breathing as Sslits carefully, slowly lay down on the air mattresses on its back. The makeshift bed creaked from the alien's enormous weight as it began to slowly re-absorb its pseudo-human feet, its legs, its hands and arms, and Billie Graham's face back into its natural amorphous state.

Unmoving and with the slightest smile on her thin lips, Celeste stood at the edge of the mattresses. She let the robe fall from her shoulders to pool on the floor around her naked feet.

The old excitement for her wasn't as intense as it had been so many years ago, but it was still there; the anticipation of new physical vitality, of the surcease of pain, of the reversal of the slow deterioration of her mind and her skin and her hair and her heart.

So she gently stepped into Sslits.

She knew it would come, and there it was; the nonsexual orgasm, the pleasurable, electric tingle racing down her legs and up her arms that some feel at the sound of a deeply loved song, or the sight of the American flag in a parade, or at the baptism of a child in a church.

Then, carefully, slowly, reverently, she lay back and began to sink into and inside the K'huprician.

Like fruit in Jell-O. A stupid thought but her's and there nevertheless.

She closed her eyes as she sank completely inside of Sslits, thinking *like a fetus inside a placenta.*

She thought *Wet. Glistening with life. Reborn. Rejuvenated. New.*

Completely immersed in the alien, the years of unrelenting conflict and anguish and fear began to melt away with the heavy creases of parchment skin, the heavy folds of flesh above slitted eyes, the pencil-thin lips, and the wrinkled forehead and yellowed hair of an eighty year old woman. Her initial terror of drowning during her first rebirth never even entered her mind this time as Celeste's lungs began to fill once more and she let her gag reflex suck in ever greater dollops of Sslits' goop until her lungs were saturated.

Then, for moments that crawled by like centuries, and as Celeste metamorphosed, she hallucinated about a cloudless sky above an unending alien desert baked dry by three enormous blood red suns, barely dimmed by night, a planet that swarmed with countless squirming amorphous bags of mucous called The Hive.

Sslits belched.

Then the alien began to sit up, trailing long lines of alien spittle from itself to Celeste, the lower part of its body still covering parts of Celeste, glistening from the mucous covering her.

As it sat up, the alien monster arduously began to regenerate its pseudo-human face and arms and legs and feet until its metamorphosis into a humanoid was complete.

Then Sslits stood for long moments next to the mattresses looking with eyes without pupils down at Celeste, watching her lungs begin to rise and fall, rise and fall, rise and fall as she lay still in profoundly deep sleep.

Celeste lay still on the glistening sheets, looking no older than thirty years of age, her eyes still closed, oblivious to the mattresses, or Sslits, or the room or anything else.

Sslits turned and sloshed out of the room.

Celeste lay on the hot, drenched sheets, now no more than twenty-two years old again, as euphoric as someone high on drugs, and opened her eyes, oblivious that…

Sslits had left the room.

CHAPTER FIFTEEN

FRIDAY, NOVEMBER 22ND, 1996, NIGHT

"**M**y goose is cooked, one way or the other," Celeste said out loud to herself, a habit learned from long stretches of isolation in labs. "Larry is going to kill me when he finds out, and he will find out. Especially since he expressly told me not to do this.

"He'll say, 'you're dead meat,' and I'll say, 'but Sslits was making such strong progress, Larry, that I just had to try this. Really.'"

Celeste Gaines was young again.

She sat, hunched forward, in a dusty, darkened room that was not in the Tribune building on a ratty folding chair overlooking the Brady District, the seldom visited and mostly abandoned clutter of two, three and four story brick and mortar buildings that stood on the north fringe of the nearby retail district of downtown Tulsa. What had once been the busy distribution hub for food and tires and furniture and clothing in the 1920s now looked like silent, dark, massive packing crates of various heights stacked and rising like irregular stairs to the sky.

She sat on the folding chair for the fourth uneventful night behind the long unwashed second story window of a warehouse that had been used to distribute automobile parts. As on each night, the former CIA agent held a pair of high powered binoculars with both hands level with her chest. And as she scanned the cityscape before her, Celeste looked like a human rubber band stretched to its emotional breaking point.

It had been like pulling teeth to find a crooked cop that would participate in the night's gambit, and had cost her a tub full of money.

Because the district was mostly abandoned, there were few street lamps, dim beneath the light from the great, yellow, gibbous moon that hung in the otherwise black, star spattered sky.

Across the street from her and defying gravity, Sslits hung naked, sexless, and face-forward, plastered to a brick wall by an adhesive squirt of its own mucous just beneath the edge of the roof of a three story building. The alien faced the more substantial cluster of skyscrapers in downtown Tulsa, alive with a randomly lit crossword puzzle of windows and the faint sounds of a spattering of traveling vehicles.

Sslits had again assumed the somewhat vague image of man as limited and warped by the alien's limited comprehension; fingers without fingernails, feet without toes, eyes without pupils—just human enough so that real men wouldn't scream in horror at first sight of the truth: three hundred gallons of muck enclosed in a 'skin' of hard water.

But Billy Graham's face had been replaced by Muhammad Ali's face and distorted by two nasty rows of savage bared teeth set in a snarl that was meant to terrorize, and the tips of its pseudo fingers had morphed into razor-sharp knives.

On its planet—where survival was everything, and to survive was to kill—violence wasn't a black and white question. It was an answer. And the answer was blood red.

Celeste raised her binoculars and swept the face of the building opposite her until; once again, she located the alien. She slowly lowered her binoculars and raised the cuff of her long-sleeved jacket to her mouth.

Into the hidden microphone at her wrist, Celeste said, "Are you there, Captain? Are you there? This is Celeste G. Is everything and everyone in place, Captain H.?"

She listened to Police Captain Hanson's response in the earpiece in her right ear. He was positioned on a side street in an unmarked police car with a clear view of the suspected target tonight, a warehouse.

"Good. Good. Remember, Hanson, no blood. I repeat, there will be no blood tonight."

She lifted the binoculars to her face and began to scan the street far below her.

As she scanned, she thought: *the image is mockery. There is no liver. There are no lungs. Hair, fingers, teeth, mouth and eyes are all lies. There is no stomach. Sslits drinks life. Absorbing moisture from the air, sucking liquid from lakes, fountains, puddles, sewers, paint cans...men. Every drop expended, a step closer to death for Sslits. But not tonight. Not tonight.*

Then Celeste caught sight of the four members of a street gang they had been expecting.

The tip to Hanson had been right.

One of the men was crouching in the open back door of a van. One of the thugs was standing on the sidewalk in front of a warehouse for a retail business in south Tulsa. A baseball bat was lying at his feet. The third thug was standing by the shop's broken plate glass window receiving a television from a forth unseen hood inside the shop. Like a fire brigade, they were passing electronic equipment to the gang member in the van.

Because of her height above the street, they looked like little male dolls.

Holding her binoculars to her eyes with her right hand, Celeste raised her wrist to her mouth again. She said, "Yeah. Hanson. Celeste again. Yeah. Okay. Everything is in place. Finally. Yeah, my ass is on the line to. Get some blues over here. Now!"

She paused to listen to his response in her ear.

"Yeah, yeah, I know. Listen, we aren't going to botch this. I'm two mil five in debt, remember? No better motive than two five. Yeah, I know; like I said, it's my butt, too."

She dropped her left hand to the binoculars and swung them up with both hands until Sslits was again in her field of vision. Releasing the binoculars with her right hand, she touched a stud on her microphone that changed its frequency.

In Sslits' head, she said, "Sslits."

She watched the alien look up as if hearing a distant voice.

She said, "Slits. Below. Stop."

Like a gigantic slug, the alien monstrosity detached itself from the wall and began to slide down the building, losing some of its human attributes and leaving a trail of mucous behind it as it did so.

As it did so, Celeste huffed and smiled. It had obeyed!

In Sslits' head, she commanded, "Sslits! Don't...kill...these. Don't kill. Make them sleep."

Celeste dropped her binoculars. She stood up from her chair and pressed her face and the palms of her hands, raised above her head, against the window's filthy glass.

She said, "These are sick hive. Make these sleep." But she had forgotten to speak into her microphone raised above her head.

She said, "Damn," and jerked her left arm down, and shouted into the microphone at her wrist, "These are sick hive. Make these sleep!! Don't kill."

As it reached the ground. Sslits regenerated the pseudo arms and legs and hands and feet it had lost in its descent.

The quartet of burglars was oblivious to the alien's presence until Sslits gurgled, *STOP*

Startled, the first of the three thugs, bald, tattooed, wearing a t-shirt and carrying an armful of television — turned, and said, "God da...!! What is that thing?!?"

He dropped the television.

The second thug in a crocheted cap said, "Ulp!"

The slaughter that followed only took seconds.

His face twisted with surprise and fear, he dropped the baseball bat studded with nails that he carried. Motivated by that same fear, he bent down and snatched the bat back up from where it lay at his feet. As he rose, he swung it up and over his shoulder above his head.

The third criminal at the van, all greasy stringy hair with a face full of stubble and metal studs and wearing an illogical pair of large sunglasses, drew a hand gun from a pocket of his leather jacket.

"Holy mutha a god," he said. "Whatever it is, it's dead."

He raised the gun and squeezed the trigger three times.

The three bullets struck Sslits in the chest and passed out its back creating little waterspouts of goo as they did so, the entrance and exit wounds sealing themselves almost instantly.

And as the first bullet struck, and although she didn't know it, Celeste's arduous, repetitious training of the alien evaporated in overwhelming, searing heat of the alien's primal instinct, an instinct shared by all life, survival.

Sslits's viscera began to bubble.

The greasy haired goon's face blanched as he said, "What th...??!! Th' bullets, man?!?"

He dropped his jaw, his hand, and the gun he held, forgotten, to his hip.

Sslits took a step forward, its right arm morphed into a ram of hard water.

Seeing that ram, and with her face and hands still pressed against the glass in the second story window overlooking the street, Celeste yelled into her microphone.

In the alien's head, Celeste yelled, "Don't kill!! Don't kill!! Don't kill, damn it!! Make these sleep!!! Sleep!!!"

Sslits swung its ram of an arm back then swung it forward with terrific force.

It slammed into the greasy-haired thug's midsection, lifting him off his feet, knocking off his sunglasses, and throwing him with terrific force against the wall of the warehouse.

His limp body fell to the sidewalk. He did not get up.

Simultaneously, the hood with the baseball bat screamed, raised the bat to strike, and lunged forward.

He screamed, "HEY, FREAK. OVVA HERE!!"

To herself and out loud, Celeste said, "Oh no, oh no, oh no."

In the alien's head, she commanded, "Sslits! Don't...kill...these!!!"

His face twisted with rage, fear, and bewilderment, the thug swung the bat with all of his strength. As he swung, the hood who had been inside the building burst out of its open front door and fled, never to be seen again.

As it passed through, the swung bat ate a chunk out of Sslits' left side.

And Sslits' viscera began to boil.

The momentum of the thug's swing spun the thief around and almost jerked him off of his feet. Sslits raised its massive left arm back.

With incredible force and speed, Sslits punched, engulfing the goon's head in its alien hand.

The thief began to choke, struggling and suffocating inside a massive glob of the alien's viscera.

High above, Celeste felt the growing rage in the alien. She whispered, "Oh, God, no."

The thief's eyes rolled back into his head.

The bald-headed thug yelled, "LENNIE!! LENNIE!!"

The baseball bat and Lennie were thrown up and back hard against their van. The nail studded bat fell, clattering, to the ground. The van dented under the impact of Lennie's body.

Lennie joined the bat.

The bald-headed thug snarled, "Back off, Man. I said back off!!"

Sslits did not back off.

The gaping wound in Sslits' side sealed itself as it turned to face the bald-headed thug.

As Sslits turned, the bald headed thief in the t-shirt pulled his gun, gripping it in both of his shaking hands. His face was a mask of horror and fear. His lips were drawn back from clenched, yellow teeth. He stuttered, "No...n-no...n-no...n-no...n-no..."

Sslits hissed *STOP*

The thug emptied his gun into the alien.

The alien's right arm and hand morphed into the long, notched blade of a scythe.

Far above, Celeste knew that all Hell was breaking loose. She dropped her binoculars and screamed into her wrist, "Sslits!!! Stop!! Sslits!!!"

Sslits slopped towards the gunman who was still pulling the trigger of his weapon although the gun was empty. Terrified, he threw the gun at the enraged alien, but missed, then illogically tried to ward off death with his now free hand.

But the image of man was shattered now. The alien will re-grow eyes, nose and tongue, and regenerate a new mockery of fingers and nails. But Sslits could not mimic a human soul. Its quasi-human face distorted with rage, devolved, its mouth disjointed, its eyes burning, and screaming in silent fury, Sslits swung the blade of the scythe back.

The bald-headed thief looked death in the face and stuttered, "No…"

Celeste yelled in the K'huprician's head: "SSLITSS!!!!"

Sslits viciously slashed the blade of the scythe in a wide arc with tremendous force.

And impaled the thief on its blade, lifting him off of his feet in a spray of blood, filling his lungs and throat and mouth with a gush of blood.

Sslits drew its blade back out of the thug's body, slick with blood.

Surprised by the intensity of her own emotions, Celeste screamed inside Sslits' head, "You mindless idiot! You killed him!! You killed him!"

At the sound of her voice in him, Sslits looked up at the window where she stood.

The thug slid off of Sslits' bloody scythe and crumpled in a sitting position to the ground.

Celeste screamed, "Do you know what will happen now!!? You screwed up everything!! You kil…Sslits. Get home!! Home! Home! NOW!!"

Celeste turned and bolted for the door of her room.

On the ground where he lay, the bald-headed thief became a corpse, unmoving, grinning,

Putrid with Sslits' mucous.

In the distance, police sirens began to wail.

The K'huprician looked up at the window where Celeste had stood, her face drained of blood, her eyes wide with fear, and said, Big Girls Don't Cry.

CHAPTER SIXTEEN

THURSDAY, NOVEMBER 8TH, 1973
KRMT RADIO, ROSWELL, NEW MEXICO

His putty soft left hand pulled the boom arm of the radio station's microphone down to his mouth as he flipped a soundless toggle switch on the control board with his right to make his microphone 'live'. In a voice that smiled, Roy said:

"Good evening, my fellow kooks and kookettes, cult cuties and conspiracy crackpots! This is Roy Koffman, and it's time for all of my fellow lunatics to howl at the moon again as I report from high atop the roof of mighty KRMT Radio because they won't let me inside the studios. I'm your host exposing the most outrageous, bizarre, supernatural, nutty, and ridiculous news, rumors, lies, and conspiracies on the airwaves, syndicated coast to coast on three – count them, three — radio stations! And every tidbit of rumor, every lie, and conspiracy is true, true, true, my true blue believers!!"

Sitting in a small office chair across from the radio announcer, Eric managed a weak smile as he struggled to hide his disgust at the pot bellied, middle-aged fool in a cowboy hat and boots that sat at the control board.

"For all of you looking for a new cult of nut K-krazies to join, we've got a special guest tonight on KRMT who is certainly beginning to gather his own little sect of true believers around him, that is, if you believe in flying saucers, little green men from outer space, and the government's conspiracy to cover it all up!"

Koffman glanced up at the huge clock on the wall in front of his control board.

"It is 10:31 p.m., and our guest tonight is the famous Mr. Eric Gaines, former CIA agent, and the only man alive whose former wife is reportedly sleeping with one of those little green things! Good evening, Eric. Welcome to the Roy Koffman Show."

"Hello, Mr. Koffman. Thank you for having me on tonight."

"Please, call me 'cupcake'! You seem a little reticent tonight. For our listeners in Podunk, Oklahoma, reticent means 'he doesn't really want to be here'. But, let me reassure you, Mr. Gaines, you will be preaching to the choir tonight. Well, at least to some kind of choir somewhere, believe you me. Are you ready?"

Koffman leaned a forearm on one of the two oversized turntables at his side that were had been used to play huge 16" vinyl transcription discs of the *Little Orphan Anne, Dick Tracy, The Shadow,* and other radio shows in the 1930s.

"We are taking phone calls from people without a television, with no life, and with nothing better to do! You know who you are, and you know the number, so get your dialing digits ready!

"Question number one: Mr. Gaines, why did you choose humble little ol' me, of all the magnificent radio personalities in New Mexico, to be the first to watch you pull the curtain back on the great and wonderful Wizard of Awe, our beneficent government, that has been hiding the truth from us all of these years?"

"KRMT was the only radio station that would have me on, Mr. Koffman."

"Ah, the old, old, story. We know it well, don't we gang? I'm talking to both you both. You know who you are.

"Fair enough, Mr. Gaines. And we don't go on formality here. You may call me 'Magnificent.'

"And just why is the government trying to cover up the existence of an alien monster that crash landed in Roswell in 1947, sir?"

"It addition to destroying the fundamental belief that the human race was created by God as the only sentient beings in the universe, certain government officials believe accurately that men always fear the unknown, and that an alien would start a panic. You know, like when radio broadcast *The War of the Worlds* back in the '30s."

"Well, I must think I must disagree, Eric. I don't think finding an alien life form would shock the world any more than when biologists find a new species of, say, turtle. But we'll just have to agree to disagree, Mr. Gaines?"

"I didn't say that I agree with the government, Roy."

"Ah, good. Now we're on a first name basis. Let's continue with what brought you here. I hold in my coffee stained fingers an issue of that apex of journalism, a grocery store tabloid titled *Global Star*. On its cover is a drawing of an alien with a head like a balloon standing on its tied-off blow hole, eyes like an owl, and two holes for a nose, no ears, and a tiny mouth. Is this an accurate drawing of the alien who supposedly landed outside of Roswell, oh so many years ago, Mr. Gaines. And why do we have no photographs of the Thing From Outer Space?"

"It is not an accurate drawing, Mr. Koffman…"

"I can't say I'm surprised."

"My wife drew that sketch to misdirect the public from the truth."

"Ah, yes, your wife. I believe the *Star* identified her as Celeste Gaines."

"Yes. At the time, she was also a CIA agent in a small office in…"

"But that isn't true?" the announcer interrupted again.

"What do you mean?"

"The article says that you are divorced now, so her last name is no longer Gaines."

"No, no, it still is Gaines. She hasn't…"

"And that you divorced her because you walked in on her in bed with the alien on Wednesday, January 5th of 1972, just about a year ago."

There was a long moment of silence as Eric's face flushed red and he balled his hands lying in his lap into fists.

"Mr. Koffman, I didn't come here tonight to talk about my private life.

I came to warn America that we stand on the brink of a real threat to America and the world, a full-fledged invasion by creatures from another world."

"No need to be testy, sir. I'm merely trying to establish your credentials as a reliable and truthful eye witness, Mr. Gaines. I believe the article further states that you have full custody of your children with Celeste. Is that because she is…well, just a bit off of her rocker?"

Eric stood up.

"Our listeners also want to know—were there also little green children and do they look like you or—well, it."

Eric stomped out of the radio station.

CHAPTER SEVENTEEN

BOSTON AVENUE BRIDGE
SATURDAY, NOVEMBER 23TH, 1996,
LATE AT NIGHT, BRADY WAREHOUSE DISTRICT

Excerpts from Celeste Gaines' Journal:

Just to rattle my chain, Odom calls Sslits "my trained dog," or, when he's trying to be particularly smart ass, My Big Red Water Balloon. And, although he knows more about my situation with Sslits than almost anyone else, he doesn't know as much as he thinks. For one thing, he doesn't know that the same device that was implanted in Sslits years ago that allows Sslits and I to "talk" is also a tracking device.

I always know where my trained dog is, so leaving my hotel room for five minutes wasn't irresponsible as Odom later claimed.

However, he was right that Sslits could not mimic a human soul.

I know because my merest touch opens the K'huprician's mind. So I knew the alien's and Lisa's destination— and followed behind her and 'my pet dog' every minute of their little adventure. It's funny, in a pathetic sort of way. My most recent training session was to see if Sslits could just make it from one end of the mall to the other without the crowds making him panic.

"ERIC STOMPED OUT OF THE RADIO STATION."

Now look at my pet dog...carrying out a secret rendezvous with this Lisa Ferry slut! How could he?! I mean it.

A television camera had taped their kiss at the mall.

When they showed it on television, they called Sslits a 'blushing hero'? For all he knew, he was French kissed by a fish. I wrote "he" again. What's wrong with me?

'He!' What a joke. Gender has no real meaning to...it.

As if waiting for Larry to show up and tear me a new one after the last disaster in the Brady district wasn't enough, now I had to put up with this. If Lisa was looking for some kind of sick sex scene — she isn't the brightest bulb on the whorehouse marquee.

•••

Lisa Ferry touched a corner of her mouth as she sat on the folding chair in Celeste's room looking in Celeste's hand-held mirror in the Tribune newspaper building. Her reflection in its mirror was marked with fear and excitement. She pursed her lips and raised a lipstick with her trembling hand to her mouth. She dropped her hand with the lipstick and smiled.

She said, "Hello, s-s-sweetie." Her voice shook as she said it.

She wore a tight little short-sleeved top with a circle cut out between her breasts. The top also left her midriff bare. She almost wore a pair of denim jeans with the legs cut off about an inch below her crotch, and nondescript sandals. Her thick hair cascaded down her back to pool on the chair.

Massive, the alien's pseudo-human face showed no emotion. Its long, colorless shock of spiked hair swept back on its head; the face beneath that faux hair looked somewhat like Clark Gable. Sslits stepped up and to the right side behind Lisa to join her reflection in the mirror.

Lisa smiled weakly. She hadn't seen Sslits naked before.

The alien gently placed its left hand on her left shoulder.

Shaking like a leaf, Lisa pushed the chair back and stood up as Sslits dropped its hand from her shoulder. She took his hand in her hand and gently squeezed it.

She said, "F-follow me, honey. We can be a-alone in my special place. No one will see us for sure."

She walked to the room's closed door with Sslits' massive hand in hers. She opened the door, stuck her head out a little, and looked first left and then right down the hallway to make sure it was empty. Celeste was not there. Then she walked Sslits down the dusty, empty hallway to the main entrance and pulled it open.

•••

A feckless yellow moon in a star spackled, cloudless sky hung over the Boston Street Bridge that had been constructed in the early 1920s. Long unsafe for vehicular traffic, the city had turned the arched bridge into a recreational walkway over two sets of two train tracks each that stretched beyond sight both East and West behind the Tribune building. It had been long decades since anything but freight trains had traveled those tracks, day or night.

Standing just around the northeast edge of the Tribune building, Celeste stood in a light windbreaker, partially hidden by the wall, her arms crossed, her face drawn with suppressed anger and her body half hidden in shadows. The few sounds of downtown Tulsa some distance behind the former agent were muted.

She bit her lower lip as she looked around the edge of the building at Sslits and Lisa silhouetted by the pock-marked moon on the pedestrian bridge just beyond her. She balled her hands into fists.

The hour was too late for casual lovers, strollers, or joggers. Sslits stood rigid and immutable in the center of the walkway. Lisa was leaning against its eastern railing. Her arms were also folded just beneath her chest; her blond hair was blown back from her face by the night's quiet breeze. They were the only two individuals on the otherwise empty walkway.

Through Sslits, Celeste heard Lisa say, "What's wrong? You're shakin' like a leaf," as she straightened from the railing to walk to the alien.

Celeste saw Lisa gently touch the alien's chin with her left hand.

Celeste jerked her left wrist up to her mouth, and shouted, "Sslits!! Don't!!"

Lisa watched the index finger of Lisa's left hand sink up to its first joint in Sslits' chin.

She said, "Oooh," as her finger sent little concentric ripples up Sslits' jaw and across the lower third of its face.

Sslits shuddered.

As pleasurable surprise morphed into electrifying shock, Lisa gasped, "Oooh!?!" and tried to jerk her finger back.

But nothing is stronger or thicker than a K'huprician's kinetic bonding.

"Oh, God!" said Lisa. "In my head! I—I can see...!"

Like alien fire, the kinetic link forged by their touching burned Sslits' primal fear into Lisa's brain — the fear of water poured into water — burned a vision of the walkway's flooring cracking, then buckling, then collapsing, and the alien falling through the gaping hole onto an overwhelming, churning body of water below that did not exist.

Clutching at the air, Sslits screamed as it fell.

Clutching at the air, Sslits screamed as it plunged into the water.

Lisa yelled, "Let...it...go!" as she struggled to jerk her finger free of Sslits' face to erase the nightmare vision out of her mind's eye of Sslits spreading like an oil spill in the illusion of river, struggling horribly, arms raised, head barely above water;

The vision of dissolution. Of assimilation, as Sslits fought to hold its liquid molecules together; of utter destruction as Sslits' head sunk below the water and its Clark Gable face, its eyes and nose and mouth, dissipated into a random pattern like oil on water.

With a herculean effort, Lisa pulled her finger out of Sslits' chin, leaving a spittle-like trail from her finger to its face.

Still in shock, she said, "What brought that on? Oh! Damn! It's afraid of water!"

As she said it, a black van skidded to a stop on Archer Street and Boston at the mouth of the walkway. Its side door was thrown open.

Lisa jerked around in the direction of the squeal of brakes.

Celeste twisted around to face the screech.

Lisa whispered, "They're heeere."

Under her breath to no one, Celeste said, "Dammit!! She's set Sslits up! It's some kind of trap!" thinking *it's Toren Walker, or the CIA, or the Russians, or, or, or...?*

It's incredible how the old agency training kicks in. As she yelled, "Sslits!!!" Celeste stuffed her right hand under her windbreaker and pulled out her old CIA service revolver. As she did so, she thought *odd they don't seem surprised or confused or afraid of what they're seeing?*

Lisa Ferry placed the palms of both of her hands on the alien's chest and pushed herself back and free.

At the same instant and one after the other, two men dressed head to toe in leather and each carrying a weapon, jumped out of the van to land heavily and flatfooted on the road.

One, grinning manically, carried an electric cattle prod with a thin steel cable running from it to a metal vest on his chest. He wore goggles over a leather skull cap.

Although she could not hear it, he said, "Get th' lead out, Robert," referring to the man carrying an undersized bazooka.

Robert answered, "Shut up, Herman."

Robert, grinding his exposed teeth, hefted the heavy bazooka up. A cable attached to the weapon ran to a metal vest across his chest. His leather cap was zippered in the middle of his skull from the back of his head to just above his nose.

A third someone in an overcoat, slouch hat, and with a scarf wrapped around the lower half of his face jumped to the road from the van to stand, unmoving, at its side. The big lapel of his overcoat was pulled up high around the sides and back of his neck.

Celeste screamed into the hidden microphone at her wrist, "SSLITS! THESE ARE BAD!!" and bolted away from the tree.

Lisa ran to the west rail of the walkway. She turned to the alien, smiled, and waved.

She cooed, "Bye-bye, baby."

She ran, full tilt, south, down the walkway.

Sslits did not move.

Celeste knew the old NIAR cliché that old agents never die because there are no old agents. She knew that, truth is, they don't all die young. They do, however, all die hard.

Knowing, she still ran at her top speed for the van.

She knew she would be seconds too late, but she ran anyway because she knew that, then again, some agents like her die hard-headed.

Herman stepped onto the walkway, he patted his cattle prod with his free hand, sneered and giggled, "Hehehe, dis gonna be fun." He snapped on the power switch of the prod that spat a web of jagged electricity at its tip.

As Celeste ran, she yelled into her wrist, "Sslits!! Make these sleep!"

The man with the hidden face did not move from the van.

Sslits stood crazy still.

Herman stopped not five feet shy of the alien who still stood, seemingly immovable and completely unaware of his presence, in the middle of the walkway.

Robert stopped ten feet short of the mouth of the walkway and raised his bazooka.

The assassin with the prod stepped two feet closer and in front of Sslits and swung the prod, crackling with raw energy, back. He giggled, "Hehehehe."

With no intonation, Sslits said, STOP.

Even as Robert saw her, Celeste skidded to a stop at his side and pressed the barrel of her service revolver on the temple of the zippered man's head.

She hissed, "I don't know who you are, but you are obviously out for blood!"

She yelled into her wrist, "Sslits!! Run!!"

She pushed the cold steel barrel of her revolver hard against Robert's temple; the grin died on his face. She hissed, "Drop it, or die!!"

The thug with the prod lunged forward and thrust the prod into the alien's massive chest.

There was hell and fire and rage in the alien's eyes and on its distorted face as the K'huprician's pseudo-lips drew back from faux fangs. Morphed into a massive club, the alien swung back its huge right arm morphed into a huge machete.

The smile vanished from Herman's face. He whispered, "Hey."

Sslits gurgled, Bye-bye baby.

Celeste yelled inside Sslits' head, "Sslits!! Don't!"

Sslits swung its machete and beheaded the thug.

Her face drained white as Celeste watched that goggled head loll in what seemed like slow motion down the walkway to stop dead at Robert's right foot.

"Mother of God!" he said, looking down at Herman's severed head. "You killed him!!?" and jerked his bazooka up.

The bazooka knocked Celeste's service revolver out of her hand and sent it flying as she stumbled backwards to fall painfully and clumsily to the road.

She screamed, "Sslits!!!" as she fell.

Sslits turned its head in the direction of her scream.

The bazooka swung down level with and to the left side of his chest.

Robert barred his teeth as he squeezed its trigger.

The shell spat from the barrel of the bazooka.

On the walkway, Sslits said, Celeste.

Celeste threw a protective arm across her face against what she knew would be the incredible percussive force of the blast.

She was right.

In a chaotic eruption of concrete, steel rods, and random debris, the bridge exploded.

CHAPTER EIGHTEEN

In the dead of night in an unnatural round clearing in the middle of a heavy copse of trees in sparsely populated north Tulsa stood the image of man in a broken mirror.

Firoz Babur, the man with the hidden face, rubbed the palms of his hands together and said, "It's show time."

Firoz was born October 16th, 1966 in the Hyderabad region of India. Child of dirt poor farmers, Firoz had been educated at a school founded by Baptist missionaries.

At twelve years old, Firoz had contracted an almost forgotten disease.

At thirty years old, he stood by a black van, idling, with its lights still on, in the middle of a denuded circle of scorched earth. Firoz was wearing a slouch hat, an overcoat, and scarf obscuring everything but his eyes. His lapel was pulled up high around the back of his neck and against the sides of his face.

The black van was parked close to the ramp that descended from a huge, silver, flying saucer in the center of the circle. Little glints of light reflecting the van's headlights randomly flashed on the spaceship's highly polished skin. The teeth of its circular dome in the center of the spacecraft looked like the mid-span supports, or blades, in a jet engine.

It was everywhere silent in the circle but for the of the motor of the idling van.

As Pariah, the Untouchable—for such was Firoz's hated nickname and his station in life—approached the ramp, he removed his hat and let it and the hand that held it fall to the side of his left hip. Then, as he ascended the ramp, he began to unwrap the scarf like medical bandages from his face.

They fell from his face like dirty ribbons of shame as he ascended the ramp, slowly revealing the horror beneath. For leprosy had eaten at his feet, his hands, and his mind. The disease had ingested his nose, an ear, and three fingers on his left hand. What limp strands of hair that were left hung from his otherwise scarred, bald skull. Firoz's upper lip had rotted away forever exposing his top row of ragged, yellowed teeth, and angry red nodules checker-boarded an otherwise fish-belly white face and destroyed his nerves, and promised certain paralysis.

It had been India's and his family's poverty and government red tape that had allowed Firoz's leprosy to continue feeding as he and his pain and his shame and his hatred grew.

It had left Firoz only one obsession.

To put on his best face.

For Firoz a pariah; a victim hungry for vengeance.

He stepped off of the ramp and through the maw of the flying saucer.

With the familiarity of long usage, Firoz walked down the saucer's perfectly smooth, circular hall that endlessly curved away from him.

He did not know if the walls were organic or inorganic, and he did not care; they no longer felt unearthly. The hallway was well lit, but by no discernible source of light. The eerie silence was broken only by the sound of his footfalls.

As he walked, he turned down the lapel from his neck and the sides of his face.

Arriving at a fork in the tube, he took the hallway on his right because he knew it curved further into the center of the craft. And, in moments, that tube opened onto a huge, circular room.

It was the stuff on nightmare.

The air was stagnant and still and unnatural. The slow drip of something heavy and liquid echoed from somewhere distant. A chaos of crossing searchlights in violent colors crawled diagonally like living things underneath and up and down its silver walls. The center of the room was a mass of cables dangling from its ceiling around a dome of some sort to an enormous chair mostly hidden by obscuring shadows.

The cables were attached to a hulking blood red thing in that chair sat hunched forward, four massive hands resting on its two pale knees.

Pariah stepped up to the foot of the chair, stopped, and knelt, his head lowered.

He said, "Master." The word echoed.

There was no response.

It had been ten years ago that the answer to his hunger had come to Firoz in the form of an alien horror searching for a traitor to its alien race... of the species Sslits of the genus K'hupric.

As he knelt, one of four gelatinous "arms" rose from a knee and stretched out from the chair to slowly engulf Pariah's head in a bubble of amorphous mucous.

To find that traitor, this Sslits, this being, this unhuman, this other Hive, needed hands, feet and a face that could move freely among human beings. Pariah needed the same. The bargain struck between the leper and the thing had been a simple one; an eye for an eye, a tooth for a tooth, a face for a face.

The gelatinous arm slopped off and back from Pariah.

Dollops of vicious mucus that had been part and partial of the horror in the chair now slowly dripped off of a face, a nose, two ears, an upper lip, and a full and lush head of hair.

Pariah lifted his left hand to his face and counted five fingers.

He whispered, "Yes, yes, yes, yes."

No red nodules checker-boarded his now clean, pink, and healthy skin.

No nerve damage paralyzed a dead white face.

Pariah shuddered with a nonsexual orgasm and smiled.

"I got good news, Spashs," he said for Spashs was what he called this Sslits.

The horror in the chair leaned forward and into a circle of yellow light around its chair.

Its sham-human head rose in a gelatinous tiara of mucous above the mockery of dead human eyes, and its tongue hung from a bear-trap of needle sharp teeth. Its four arms ending in clawed hands writhed like snakes from a torso covered with blisters of tiny, bleached human skulls. Grey cobra-shaped welts circled its ankles and wrists, and a skirt of pseudo-human arms and hands hung like a skirt around its faux hips.

Indifferent from long familiarity, smug and confident, Pariah said "Sslits is dead."

A light from the dome above the repulsive slop snapped on.

The thing in the chair hissed.

It did not look like Billy Graham.

As if poorly realized by a half-blind mad artist, it looked like Kali, the Hindu Goddess of Death and Destruction.

CHAPTER NINETEEN

TUESDAY, APRIL 8TH, 1975, 10:03AM
ABC NETWORK STUDIOS, 77 W 66TH ST STE 100
NEW YORK CITY, NEW YORK

Eric Gaines had finally hit the Big Time.

Everything about ABC News, its lobby, the long hall flanked by plush offices, even the waiting room, were top notch and a far cry from the weary little radio stations in small towns, the regional television studios with reporters and news personalities all pretending to be a big deal, and the understaffed, cluttered newspaper offices that had been the backdrop for most of his life for decades.

He wasn't surprised that the young woman who came to get him from the waiting room was impeccably and expensively dressed in a white blouse and black skirt. It was, however, somewhat unnerving that she looked a bit like Celeste did almost thirty years ago.

Eric followed her out of the waiting room and down the hall past the main studio from which the national news was broadcast without hesitation. He knew that he was here to be filmed for an ABC special on the history of UFOs in America. He also knew he was there to be exploited for ratings and nothing else.

Even at fifty-three and with his terrible experiences with women, he still watched the rhythmic sway of his hostess's hips as she preceded him down the hall.

But he was a bit surprised at how small the studio was where he would be filmed. It wasn't more than twenty feet by twenty feet, if that. In its center stood two chairs. They did look comfortable. Two bulky television cameras were placed about five feet in front of the chairs, and a small canvas folding chair had been placed to the left of the cameras.

His hostess walked him to one of the two chairs in the room, and left with a polite thank you and no more. As she returned to the only door, four men passed her as they entered. Only one of the men smiled at her.

Eric recognized Kris Bernham from the many ABC specials he had hosted. Probably in his late thirties, Kris was trim, even athletic, and clean shaven, with conservatively cut black hair, and enough pancake makeup to eat breakfast off of his face. He wore a very expensive, gray suit. When they walked directly to their equipment, it became obvious to Gaines that two of the other ABC employees were the cameramen for the shoot. The fourth man sat in the canvas chair used by directors in every film Eric had ever seen.

Eric stood as Bernham reached him and extended his hand to the newsman. Bernham shook his hand and smiled a toothy grin.

He said, "Hello, Mr. Gaines. It's so nice to meet you."

Eric said, "You also."

Bernham said, "Please be seated," and took his own advice as Eric sat.

"You do understand that this is being prerecorded for broadcast at a later date."

"Of course," responded Eric. "I read the contract and signed it."

"Yes, yes, of course. Then I guess we are ready."

He nodded at the director who returned the newsman's nod with one of his own.

The director raised a hand without looking at the cameras and said, "Let's roll film."

Kris said, "We are talking with world renowned UFOlogist Eric Gaines who some call the granddaddy of all of those people across America who keep their eyes on the skies. Not only has he been frequently in the news for three decades or so when the news was about little green men from Mars, he is also the most controversial of his peers because he has often debunked much of the 'evidence' used to prove his own belief. Is that a fair characterization, Mr. Gaines?"

"Not really, Mr. Bernham…"

"Please, call me Kris."

"I am also a former CIA agent trained in all of the techniques used in investigation whose credentials as such were never questioned. I do not believe in 'little green men from Mars' because the one alien that is now on Earth is not little, is not green, is not a man, and is not from Mars. As for debunking some of the evidence used to prove the existence of flying saucers and aliens, I am all about finding and defending the truth."

"I am a little confused by your last statement, Mr. Gaines. As one of the most ardent supporters of the existence of alien life visiting Earth, are you saying that many of the reports of flying saucers, alien abductions, and such are false, and, if so, what is responsible for these false reports."

Eric leaned forward in his chair. "The crash of a flying saucer near Roswell, New Mexico, in 1947 was real, as was the alien that survived that crash. The rest of it was all fabricated by obscure men and women wanting the publicity and fame that comes with these reports, or by our own government. In fact, the government has been behind most of the false reports since 1947. They have 'set them up and knocked them down' to create a culture of skepticism to try to suppress the truth."

"Are you claiming that all of the film clips, the hardback and paperback books, the movies about aliens invading earth, the hard evidence of alien metals, etc., have all been staged by our own government to obfuscate the truth?"

"Absolutely."

"And have you brought your own hard evidence with you today to support your accusations, Mr. Gaines? Do you have photographs, film clips, or other physical evidence that will prove alien life on our planet?"

There was a long and painful pause.

Eric said, "No.

"But I am working on it, and am close to being able to do so soon."

Bernham said, "I see," that was followed by another painfully long pause.

"Then why did *you* agree to appear on a segment of our 'UFO: Fact or Fiction" special, Mr. Gaines?"

Eric answered, "I am proud to announce the long overdue creation of an organization of like minded people from all over the world who are dedicated to one cause and one cause only. The creation of this organization will allow me to raise the funds necessary to find and present absolutely concrete evidence that at least one alien is alive and in America even as we speak.

"As of today, the Americans Against Insterstellar Migration has earned non-profit standing and is, so to speak, open for business"

Bernham smiled and asked, "And what is the goal of the Americans Against Interstellar Migration, Mr. Gaines?"

"You may call it AAIM, if you wish, Mr. Bernham. That is a bit easier to remember. Our purpose is to dedicate ourselves to spread the word that there are aliens, that there is already one entrenched on Earth at this very moment, and that they will stop at nothing in accomplishing their agenda."

"They have an agenda? And what is that agenda, Mr. Gaines?"

"The invasion and conquest of the world."

Eric turned at the sound of the snigger to see one of the cameramen trying to suppress his laughter behind the hand cupped over his mouth.

The director jumped up from his canvas folding chair, and barked, "Cut! Cut! Who the hell laughed?"

Bernham answered, "Johnnie, our cameraman."

The director stomped over to Johnnie and intense but whispered words were exchanged. The smile faded from the cameraman's face, replaced by somber submission.

Shaking his head in disbelief, the director returned to his chair, and sat down.

"I am terribly sorry for that unprofessional outburst, Mr. Gaines. But I'm sure you'll understand that we can't use that last statement with laughter behind it. It was a great line, and your expression was just perfect. Could I ask you to repeat it from the top?"

Eric had endured decades of derision and worse, and his natural response would have been a burst of anger painted with profanity, but he swallowed his pride and firmed his resolve. He would endure anything to poke a finger in Celeste's eye.

He began again, "AAIM's goal is to inform the world…"

CHAPTER TWENTY

BOSTON AVENUE BRIDGE
SATURDAY, NOVEMBER 23TH, 1996,
LATE AT NIGHT, DOWNTOWN TULSA

In 1947, the image of God as reflected in an alien mirror fell to earth.

That image was transformed into rumors of little green men, of alien invasions and government cover-up.

It was all a very neat little package. But then the mirror blew up.

Celeste's face drained of blood as she watched Herman's goggled head loll in slow motion down to and through the mouth of the walkway to stop dead at Robert's right foot.

"Mother of God!" the hit man said, looking down at Herman's bloody face, his unblinking eyes that were staring up at Robert were filled with terror. "You killed him!" Robert added and jerked his bazooka up.

The bazooka swatted Celeste's service revolver out of her hand and sent it flying as she stumbled backwards to fall painfully to the road.

She screamed, "Sslits!!!" as she fell.

Sslits turned his head in the direction of the scream.

Robert's bazooka swung down level with and to the left side of his chest.

Robert barred his teeth as he squeezed its trigger.

The shell spat from the barrel of the bazooka.

On the walkway, Sslits said, Celeste as Celeste threw a protective arm across her face against what she knew would be the incredible percussive force of the blast.

She was right.

She curled into a tight ball.

In a chaotic eruption of concrete, steel rods, and random debris, the bridge exploded.

"SSLITS!" Celeste yelled for no other reason than to release the horror knotted in a ball in her stomach.

As she yelled, a temporary superheated red and yellow fireball shot up into the night sky above an instantaneous, jagged, gaping hole in the left side of the walkway, followed by a churning black ball of smoke obscuring the spot where Sslits had stood.

Celeste cautiously dropped her arms from her face and pushed herself up into a kneeling position. The sky was still slowly drizzling bits of charred debris. The flames from the walkway under-painted her face with dancing shadows. She glanced to her right side.

His head crushed under a concrete chunk torn out of the walkway and thrown by the concussion of the explosion, Robert lay dead by her side.

Celeste struggled to her feet, shielding her face from the falling debris with her left hand, and immediately began to trot to the mouth of the walkway.

As she ran, she choked, "Oh God, oh God, h-he's...dead."

Caution thrown to the wind, she ran up the walkway, only slowing as she approached the gaping hole in its southernmost railing and floor.

Her pace faltered and she stopped cold as she saw nothing where Herman and Sslits only moments ago were tearing at one another.

She would later learn in a sensationalist report on the evening news of a local television station that Herman's shattered body had been blown off of the bridge onto the tracks below.

Great gobs of Sslits had been bestrewn, splattered, all over the walkway.

She sank to her knees, and said, "H-h-he's....g-gone...."

But it was not Celeste Gaines who began to sob like a baby. It was Celeste Jones, the little girl who had screamed "Mitsy!!" as she fell to her knees in front of the broken bones, bloody fur, heaving chest, and whimper that was left behind of her beloved dog in Byng.

It was the little girl who had rocked back and forth as she cradled Mitsy's bloody head in her lap, sobbing as Mitsy, panting heavily, gurgled unnaturally in her throat.

It was Celeste Jones who hugged Mitsy to her chest as the dog's life seeped out in red tears until her ruptured heart stopped beating and her chest stopped heaving and her beautiful black eyes glazed over and her best friend in the whole world shuddered and died.

So, her eyes blinded by tears, Celeste did not see the gobs of alien mucous stir and crawl, slowly and almost soundlessly, down and off of the protective railing and across the walkway, gathering.

And deafened by her own sobbing, Celeste did not hear as an alien blob conjoined, converged, collected itself and slowly rose up behind her in an eldritch wave.

But she did fell the massive alien hand on her shoulder.

She looked up and gasped, stunned, and overjoyed.

Sslits placed his massive hands on both of her shoulders and lifted her up to her feet from the walkway.

Stuttering from emotion, Celeste said, "Sslits!!! Y-y-you're *alive*?!!! Alive!!! I thought you were..."

Sslits gurgled, Big Girls Don't Cry.

Celeste buried her face against the alien's 'chest'.

After a long moment there, she leaned back and away a bit against the alien's embrace and said, "Sslits! I think Toren Walker tried to kill you!"

Sslits shook its head no.

Its 'face' emotionless, the alien hissed, *Spashs are here.*

SATURDAY, NOVEMBER 23TH, 1996, SECLUDED WOOD NORTH OF TULSA

Pariah lifted his left hand in front of his face and counted five fingers.

He whispered, "Yes, yes, yes, yes, yes."

He placed his five fingers on his left cheek.

Red and brown scabs no longer checker-boarded his now clean, pink, and healthy skin. No nerve damage paralyzed his dead, white face.

Pariah shuddered with a nonsexual orgasm and smiled.

He was clean again.

"I got good news, Spashs," he said.

The horror in the chair leaned forward.

Smug and confident, Pariah said "Sslits is dead*!*"

The thing in the chair hissed *Aaaaaahhhhh*

"Sslits is dead," Pariah repeated. "Dead, Spashs!"

Spashs slobbered, *Come closer Pariah*

Pariah moved two steps closer to the horror.

Sslits   Spashs are Hive, hissed Spashs. *Yes Sslits are scouts   sslits failed   sslits must die."*

"S-spashs..." said Pariah. "I don't...?"

One of its four gelatinous arms snailed in slow motion out to Parish's shoulder as if to comfort the leper as it said,

Spashs judges.

Does pariahs think Spashs stupid?

Its gelatinous arm again fell onto Pariah's head in a glop of amorphous mucous.

Pariah's scream became a gurgle.

Its massive, gelatinous arm slowly engulfed Pariah's neck and shoulders in amorphous red mucous.

Sslits not dead.

Pariah twisted and lurched inside the gelatinous dollop as he began to drown.

Pariahs fails.

Pariah fell on his knees, his hands clutching, tearing at the amorphous mucous that engulfed his head and sucked out health, sanity, and life from his convulsing body.

For leprosy again ate at his feet, his hands, his mind, was chewing off his nose, an ear, and three fingers on his left hand. Limp strands of hair again hung from his otherwise scarred, bald skull, and Firoz's upper lip rotted away, exposing ragged, yellowed teeth. Angry red nodules checker-boarded his fish-belly white face and deadened his skin, and destroyed his nerves.

Its elongated, slimy tongue snaked out of Spashs' contorted leering face and licked its 'lips' as it gurgled:

So leprosy eats pariahs again.

The alien jerked its hand from Firoz's head.

Firoz fell to the floor.

Spashs hissed, *now Spashs kills Sslits.*

CHAPTER TWENTY ONE
TUESDAY, NOVEMBER 26, 1996
DOWNTOWN TULSA, PEDESTRIAN MALL

As was her habit, Celeste said out loud to herself, "Ignorance is bliss, eh, Larry?" while thinking *thank god Hanson kept the lid on so far knock on wood.*

Celeste had a multitude of reasons for being nervous as she stood in the middle of Tulsa's Pedestrian Mall in downtown Tulsa, shifting her weight from one foot to the other and biting the fingernail of the first digit of her left hand, waiting for the film to roll.

Because she and Police Captain Hanson both had to do double duty to watch each other's backs due to the botched experiment with the burglars in the Brady District, the policeman had hired a dozen or so off-duty policemen for security. They were positioned at very point of ingress and egress to the mall that had also been cordoned off from the general public.

She added out loud to herself, "And thank God he doesn't know about the bridge either," while thinking *for such a smart guy, Larry really doesn't have a clue.*

The advertising agency had secured the permit to seal off the main mall for two hours during the commercial shoot. The new Lincoln Continental was already parked in the middle of the mall, and three women, as nude as the law would allow, were fidgeting on its roof.

Three cameras, cameramen, the director, and a battery of portable klieg lights were in place in a half-arc around the east side of the new automobile.

Celeste bit the fingernail of a digit of her left hand as she looked around the perimeter of the somewhat absurd scene, and thought, *for fifteen years, even* attempts *to just communicate with Sslits failed as rumors grew into myth—certainly, Big Brother had had a hand in turning those rumors into myth, and the NIAR had deliberately expanded the myth into legend. And now I'm going to blow up the myths just for money? So, whose the bigger idiot?*

The rumors had become myths, and the myths had become legends that spawned cheap sci-fi drive-in movies, boiled over into comic books, Rock 'n Roll and the Captain Video television show, morphed into lurid paperback exposes, toy ray guns and lunch boxes…and television commercials about women in bikinis on top of Continentals.

Out loud, she said, "Oh, brother," even as she reflected on the past decades, and thought with resignation, *Such is life; such is alien life.*

By 1973, the government had long claimed ownership of the thing codenamed B.L.O.O.D.T.I.D.E on grounds of national security in a series of secretive, legal battles. But after fourteen years in closed military trials, Celeste had won the first go-around of her countersuit through the law firm of McCormick Eaton Myers and Odom by successful arguing that Sslits was a sentient being.

She wondered if the girls on the car would think so when they saw the alien.

" CELESTE ... WAITED FOR THE FILM TO ROLL. "

The government, Celeste, and the growing movement behind her ex-husband's lunatic, fringe group, AAIM, all knew that the suit and countersuit were bogus, a tissue of lies. No one really believed the American people followed by the rest of the peoples of the world would panic upon learning that humans were not the only sentient life form in the universe. Nor had the first such lawsuit been the only one.

And, of course, Celeste knew the original suits were bogus because she had 'accidentally' fallen into the K'huprician and knew the truth better than anyone. Plunged right inside his 'liquid' body. That was when Celeste at first and miraculously become young again.

That's why she looked all of thirty years old as she stood impatiently in the Pedestrian Mall when she was actually eighty years old.

Out loud, looking with disdain at the models on the car, she said, "Bimbos" as she thought *I'd give my left arm to look like that.*

A secret like that is impossible to keep, and the truth of her new youth spread slowly at first, and then like wildfire, first, through those directly connected with B.L.O.O.T.I.D.E, then through family, friends and associates, and then through the general population as part of the myth of little green men. After all, everyone wants to live forever. Even cold and calculating scientists yearn for eternal youth. So Sslits' "value" doubled, then tripled, then quadrupled among those few who knew it existed.

Celeste's only protection through the legal wrangling had been Larry Odom; her knight-in-armor had been her lawyer-in-a-shark-skin-suit.

Lawsuits and lawyers don't come cheap. So when the advertising agency of *Tiger, Davis, Fortier and Rosenblum*, a.k.a. *Airship Advertising*, had approached Celeste in November of 1995 with an offer of $250,000 and residuals if she could produce the alien to be filmed for a national television commercial, her overwhelming need to raise funds to cover those legal fees won out over every concern she felt even now.

She shifted her weight from her right to her left leg.

The advertising agency and Lincoln Continental were gambling that not only would they produce the most watched commercial in the history of advertising, they would win unbelievable publicity in being the first to film and therefore prove that an alien from another world not only existed…but drove a Lincoln.

As she waited impatiently for the crew to begin filming, Celeste was not oblivious to the fact that she betting everything. It was just another reason why she was sweating bullets.

She was gambling big-time that the residuals would be enormous. She

SSLITS

was betting that the public would not panic at its first actual glimpse of an alien. Maybe they'd think the K'huprician was animation. And, as icing on her cake, she was gambling that she would also outsmart her ex-husband again by releasing proof of Sslits existence before he and his crazy A.A.I.M. organization could do so.

The logistics, however, had been daunting.

Celeste stood in the middle of the outside mall in downtown Tulsa scanning the rows of windows in the buildings that towered above and on every side of her. She searched those windows for a camera or for a rifle. A camera other than those owned by the advertising agency could destroy her fee and residuals; she didn't worry about bullets killing Sslits. They would pass harmless through the alien. Bullets would not, however, pass harmlessly through her or anyone else involved in what could be a fiasco.

As she scanned the buildings, she held a Walkie-talkie in her right hand to communicate with Larry Odom, who was waiting in their white van in the mouth of a side street ready to produce Sslits for filming at Celeste's signal, or with Captain Hanson.

She raised the Walkie-talkie to her mouth, pressed a stud, and said, "Looks all clear, Larry. Are you ready?"

Odom responded, "Ready. At your signal, I'll hold my talkie in front of its face and say, "Go, Lassie, go boy!"

The sneer in her response was obvious. "Very funny, Larry. Remind me to laugh just before I fire you."

"Stick and stones, Celeste; stick and stones."

She pressed the stud on the Walkie-talkie again, and said, "Ready, Captain?"

Hanson replied, "Affirmative."

She pressed the stud on her Walkie-talkie and said, "Larry, send 'My Favorite Martian.'"

Celeste sighed and re-attached the Walkie-talkie to her belt. She was only somewhat confident that all of her dominoes were in place and that they would fall at the right time. Now it was all in the hands of Fate or the God that she was uncertain even existed.

Odom jumped out of the driver's side of the van, trotted to its rear, and opened the double doors on Sslits, sitting immobile and indifferent on the floor.

Celeste raised her wrist and spoke into the microphone hidden there and into Sslits' head. She said, "Sslits, come."

Sslits rose up, losing and then regaining its human form looking somewhat like muscle-builder Charles Atlas as it did so. It slowly oozed out of the van onto the street and began to follow as Odom, looking over his shoulder as he did so, waved it forward.

The commercial's director and crew and the women on the automobile instinctively recoiled, drawing back, as they watched it flow up to the Lincoln Continental.

Obviously nervous, the director said, "We can't miss this shot, gang. Keep on your toes."

As Sslits stood by the Lincoln Continental, Celeste spoke into her wrist microphone.

"Sslits, under the car. Then lift and stand still."

The alien collapsed into a mound of goo that slowly roiled under the car.

The director snapped, "Roll!"

The car, slightly rocking from side to side, rose up.

And up, and up, and up.

The three models on its roof fought for balance while trying to smile.

Sslits stood up, straining, as it balanced the car on its shoulders over its lowered head.

Larry Odom joined Celeste, watching the scene with open trepidation and disgust.

He pulled out a cigarette from his shirt pocket and lit it.

As he inhaled, Celeste said, "Cigarettes will kill you, Larry. There are days that I would welcome that. But not today."

Larry said, "So will an exclusively liquid diet, honey."

Celeste ignored Odom as she chewed a fingernail.

CHAPTER TWENTY TWO

"It's been some wild, wild ride, kiddo," continued the lawyer as he scanned the buildings and the area around the commercial shoot. "The big slug saves a woman falling to her death in a Tulsa mall and becomes a hero...."

Celeste interrupted, "Don't start, Larry. I'm not in the mood today."

"Then," continued Larry, "you, sweet Celeste, get a major face lift and tummy tuck that would make any starlet in Hollywood envious, shaving years off your age..."

"Did you not hear me, Larry? Shut up."

"...again."

The three near naked models on the roof of the Lincoln had gained their balance now and were pretending that they were in love with the automobile.

Odom inhaled cigarette smoke deeply into his lungs. He exhaled.

"C'mon, Celeste. When do you start seeing the insanity in all of this?"

"And you know that Sslits has no human concept of time or space or even how natural law works on Earth except what it has learned in the last two decades. Sslits is totally instinctual; its first and only concern is survival. You also know Sslits has no concept of right and wrong, much less of anything approaching love," Celeste continued. "So, as a completely alien being, Sslits can't be held responsible for anything."

Larry took his cigarette out of his mouth and blew a smoke ring into the air. "Oh," he said, "he's not responsible, Celeste.

"You are.

"And, don't look now, but someone with a big freaking camera and a tripod has snuck under the cordoning tape."

Both watched as a middle-aged, red-headed man who now stood on their side of the tape that cordoned off the area raised a heavy camera to his shoulder.

Before he could push a button, however, two policemen ran to his side.

"Know why I put up with all of this?" asked Larry as he watched the scene unfold. "It's the money, pure and simple. Big money, I might add. But, for the life of me, outside of your occasional beauty bath inside Sslits..."

"One more word, Larry, and I hire Perry Mason."

Both continued to watch, now much concerned, as an argument began to get heated between the red-headed man and the police.

"Celeste, Celeste, Celeste, I have no real earthly idea why you really stick with our freakish, uh, friend."

"Sure you do, Larry. I was loved and believed in everything my mom and pop taught me. I was baptized at eight by Pop. Girl scouts. Class president, high school and college. No drugs, no drinking. Young Republicans. Voted.

"Married, although still a virgin at twenty. Never cheated. Loved Eric and my two kids. And God and country. I was and am a straight arrow, Larry. I'm a scientist who believes all life is sacred. Even the lives of lawyers. That's why I stick with Sslits."

Neither could hear a single word spoken as Celeste and Odom watched the policemen shove the red-headed cameraman back under the tape and ordered him away from the shoot by pantomime with extended arms and pointed fingers. From the cameraman's expression, they could tell the redhead was no happy camper as he skulked away.

"The only person I've ever met," said Larry, "who really believes in truth, justice and the American Way. Saint Celeste."

"You make my skin itch."

"You'll get over it. Lawyers and snakes shed their skins every year or so anyway."

"You know," continued Larry, "this Sslits thing is an insurmountable legal mess, even for the distinguished law firm of McCormick Eaton Myers and Odom."

The director shouted "cut"!

Celeste spoke into the hidden microphone at her wrist and into Sslits head.

"Slowly. Slowly. Put the car down. Return to van."

The Lincoln Continental began to sink back to the street as Sslits devolved back into a mound of goo again, and oozed out from beneath the luxury car. Then Sslits rose up by the side of the automobile, losing and then regaining its human form.

It looked somewhat like Marilyn Monroe.

Celeste shook her head in resignation and said, "I'll walk you two back at the van."

•••

As Celeste and Larry spoke below him, an old man sat behind a third story, fly speckled window overlooking the Pedestrian Mall. His face wore the age and wear of seventy-four years and the intensity of obsession. He sat in a wheelchair in a room cast deep in shadow; his face looking like it had been furrowed with a rake. His blue-veined hands trembled slightly as he held a pair of black, high-powered binoculars made of a pimpled metal to his eyes. A small yellow blanket covered his legs below his waist that fell loosely to his ankles. He leaned forward in his wheelchair to watch as Celeste Gaines and Larry Odom joined Sslits and began to lead the shambling alien back to their van.

The furrowed man's deep concentration was broken only by the sound of the room's door opening behind him.

The redheaded man with the camera who was in the Mall moments before stood in the doorway, backlit by the light in the hallway behind him. His name was Don Richmond.

He asked, "I guess you saw, sir?"

The old man lowered his field binoculars.

"Yes, yes, I'm afraid I did, Don. But don't let it disturb you. It wasn't a total loss."

As the handicapped man began to swing his wheelchair around to face the redhead, Don Richmond said, "I couldn't do much of anything with those two cops on my back."

The furrowed man laid his binoculars in his lap. "Let's count our blessings, Don. At least our contact was right; Sslits was here. It's a shame our contact didn't also tell us it was at a photo shoot, but it turns out that luck was with us, and that worked to our advantage. True, we came this close," he raised a hand and parted his thumb and index finger a sixth of an inch apart, "to getting the photographic proof of the existence of that alien monstrosity that A.A.I.M. has wanted for decades.

"But, it is apparent that an advertising agency has done the job for us, and will give us more immediate and national exposure than we could have hoped for, Don, with our film. So, today has been a win-win for us, don't you think?

"Hit the light switch for me, will you?"

Don flipped the light switch next to the door up and stepped inside the room.

He asked, "Isn't it about time that I know the name of our contact, Mr. Gaines? After all, by your own design, I'm your chosen head for AAIM when you're...well, you know, when it's time."

"That's still for me to know and you not to, I'm afraid. Just be patient, son. Everything in its own good time."

The furrowed old man in the wheelchair smiled.

"I think I'd like to look at it again, Don. Could you bring it out of the room over there?" he said pointing with a bony finger.

Hesitant, Richmond asked, "Do you think that's really wise, Mr. Gaines? Someone might just walk in and see it."

The old man dismissed Richmond's comment with a wave of his blue veined hand.

"The whole world will see it soon enough, Don. Wheel it out, please."

It was a polite command, not a question, and Richmond knew it.

He walked to the door on the south side of the room, opened it, and stepped through, leaving the door open behind him. The thin squeaking of un-oiled metal wheels on the room's tiled floor preceded the little metal cart that Don pushed before him towards Gaines. A heavy, white cloth draped over something conical hung half way down to those protesting wheels.

Richmond pushed it in front of the old man, stopped, and stood, waiting for instructions.

The old man rubbed his blue veined hands together as he said, "It's been almost fifty years since my ex-wife showed me the little film about our little treasure on that cart, Don. Fifty years. Too damn long. It's been almost that long since the man who stole it from Roswell sold it to the Russians for a king's ransom. Take off the cloth, son."

Richmond asked, "You never told me, Mr. Gaines. Who was the thief?" He jerked the cloth off of the cart and let it fall on the floor.

"No one knows, Don," Gaines lied. "No one knows."

On the cart lay an odd patchwork of metal struts holding a cylinder easily four feet long that looked like a huge, silver twist of licorice.

Don said, "You did really pull off a coup with this one, Mr. Gaines."

"If the Russians had ever figured out how to use it, I wouldn't have it now, Don. Even at that, it took more than twenty years to raise enough money through AAIM to buy it. Twenty long, dead, years. Twenty years of being ridiculed, called a lunatic, a madman. But Celeste made one of the biggest mistakes of her life when she showed me the surveillance tape from the lab in Roswell, back when we were still talking, that the Russians never saw."

The old man wheeled his chair up to the silver cylinder and raised his right hand just above its surface. There were beads of sweat on his forehead, and his eyes were bright.

"He destroyed my marriage and my career, Don. It is because of that queer piece of alien crap that ninety percent of the population thinks you and I and AAIM are crackpots, at best, and idiots, at worst. He has made my life a living hell."

"He,sir?"

"I meant 'it.' You know that. Outside of the alien maggot they call Sslits, Celeste and I are the only two people in the world who know how to fire it."

The old man patted the alien weapon.

"And when I discharge it…"

His hand began to shake.

He patted the alien weapon.

"Sslits will evaporate like a drop of water hitting a hot skillet."

The old man let his hand fall to the arm of the wheelchair.

"And I will be free."

The old furrowed man was Eric Gaines.

CHAPTER TWENTY THREE

Odom opened the back doors of their van.

Celeste said, "Sslits. Get in."

Sslits took a step toward the van and stopped between the two opened doors. The lawyer took a prolonged drag on his cigarette. His face was lined with a mix of anger and worry.

"That went way too easily," he said. He let his still burning Camel cigarette fall to the ground at his feet. "When that commercial breaks, Celeste, all Hell will break loose. I haven't the slightest idea of how to handle that. Maybe I should just blow my brains out now and be done with this whole thing."

"I'd help you, Larry, but, my pea-shooter's at home."

A disembodied voice behind them said, "I'd offer to, Lar, but mine doesn't shoot peas."

Celeste and Larry turned to the sound to see six men standing behind them. Five of the men wore military uniforms and side arms. The sixth man was Police Captain Hanson.

Celeste said, "Wood. What an expected pleasure. You're enough to make a person wish that Toren Walker hadn't retired. What brings you to this neck of the Wood...besides Police Captain Hanson? Did they run out of prostitutes at the NIAR, Charlie?"

Lieutenant General Charles Wood took a step in front of the other five men and said, "Not all that clever an insult, Celeste. In fact, that's sort of a smutty remark for 'Saint Celeste' to make, isn't it, dear?"

Celeste said, "So how much did it take to buy you off, Hanson?"

The Police Captain said nothing.

Odom said, "What do you want, Mr. Wood," his tone of voice not indicating a question. "I'm sure you can see we're kind of busy here at the moment."

"Lieutenant General to you, Mr. Odom. I'm here to deliver a message or an ultimatum, depending on one's viewpoint, I guess, that doesn't really concern Celeste's mouthpiece."

"I prefer legal representative. So deliver it," sneered Larry. "We won't stand on legal formalities for the moment; just like you."

Celeste began to raise her wrist to her mouth.

Wood slapped his sidearm on his hip with his right hand.

"I wouldn't advise that, Mrs. Gaines. You'll notice that my men are wearing side arms, and, on closer inspection, you'll also notice that each is carrying several high concussion grenades on his belt.

"If you sic that thing on me, you and I both know that I may not be able to kill that abomination you've spent the last couple of decades protecting, but my men can sure scatter gobs of it all over the mall for enough time for me to do what I came to do."

With measured tone and suppressed anger, Celeste said, "I was simply going to tell Sslits to get in the van and sit down."

There was a tense moment of silence in which Wood would have sworn one of his men behind him snickered.

"Oh," he said. "That sounds like a good idea."

Celeste spoke into her wrist. The van sank perceptively under the alien's weight as Odom took a prolonged drag on a new cigarette. His face was lined with anger and worry.

"Celeste, as your legal counsel, I advise you to say or do nothing…" Odom began.

"Give it up, Larry," Celeste interrupted. "Resistance never works. I'm curious to hear their lies about their river walk fiasco, anyway."

Larry interrupted, "What river walk fiasco?"

Ignoring the lawyer, Wood shifted his weight to his left foot. "Ah, that. Your paranoia has no limits, has it, sugar. That wasn't us. But we were there; we are always there. And it sure made an interesting show. We'd like to know who was behind as well. And that little fiasco is one of the reasons I'm here today.

"You've finally stepped over the line…"

Odom barked, "You do or try anything without a court order in your stinking hand and I'll have NIAR crawling with media within thirty minutes, Wood!!"

"Thanks for the warning. We'll wear make-up.

"The foolishness at the bridge the other night and this nonsense of having that alien maggot filmed for commercial release broke the camel's back, Celeste."

Larry interrupted, "What bridge foolishness?"

Wood reached into a breast pocket on his uniform and took out a tri-folded paper.

He said, "We obviously can't take you or that thing into custody here because of the danger of that maggot infested water balloon hurting someone, but you are hereby ordered to appear before a judicial panel of the NIAR on Tuesday, November 26th at 2:00 p.m."

Wood tried to hand the paper to Celeste as Odom stepped quickly in between them.

He said, "That's a fake summons, Celeste; don't touch it. There is no such thing as a 'judicial panel' of the NIAR. And what have you got to do with the NIAR anyway, Wood? This whole thing is beginning to stink."

The smile on Celeste's face was cold and full of suppressed anger as she said, "After following us around for years with little plastic buckets and shovels collecting Sslits droplets for study, I'd have thought you knew everything that there was to know about my 'pet dog', Wood, and about me as well. I don't bend over backwards for you or anyone else."

She waved Odom back as Wood replaced the paper in his pocket.

"You are making a grave mistake, Mrs. Gaines. If you don't appear, we'll bring you and that slime bag in by force, if necessary."

Celeste shook her head in mock disappointment.

"Why don't you hand me another summons again twenty years from now when your final appeal fails, eh, Charlie?" She glanced at Sslits, motionless and emotionless, in the van.

"Oh, dear, I forgot....You won't be able to, Charlie. I'll still be twenty-five years old and you'll be dead by then."

Wood's face blanched and he clenched his left fist.

Celeste continued, "Let's get down to brass knuckles, shall we, Charlie? The real reason you are here, there, and everywhere I go is that your lab boys know the alien's chemical makeup is what makes me forever young. And you want forever young."

Wood snapped, "That's a disgusting lie!! You stopped the most important—the only—research into an alien life form in history!!"

"I'm twenty-five," sneered Celeste. "You're getting old and dying."

"Bitch."

"And you smell bad too."

Wood drew his right hand back and swung it backhanding Celeste with some force. Odom lunged forward, but stopped. Several of Wood's men raised hands just above their side arms, and Hanson barked, "Wood!!"

"Uuh!" Celeste grunted as she staggered back a foot, blinding drops of light exploding in her head. As she placed a hand against her cheek, she saw Sslits rise up in the van.

The van rose perceptively without the alien's weight as Sslits roared out of its open back doors, its quasi-human face distorted with rage, its mouth disjointed, its eyes burning, and screaming in silent fury.

Before she could lift her face, before a single hand could draw a side arm, as "Bitch" still lingered on Wood's mouth, the K'huprician's great right hand grabbed Wood by his throat and jerked the Lieutenant General off his feet, gasping for air.

The alien hissed *WOOD* and effortlessly tossed the man aside.

Wood struck the interior of the open right door of the van and fell to the street in a jumble of twisted arms and legs like a broken puppet.

"S-SLITS!!" Celeste commanded, "STOP!!" as the blinding light in her head fell apart into a swirl of dissipating embers and the false vision of Sslits coming to her rescue, of the alien killing Wood, dissipated with the burned-out ashes of light.

Celeste looked up at Wood, his rage melting into shame, the hand with which he had slapped her hanging loosely at his side.

She looked inside the van and somewhere beneath conscious thought, long buried with the little girl named Celeste Jones, a little girl's eyes welled with tears because her alien knight in shining armor sat in the van...

Emotionless and immobile.

Odom stepped up.

"Enough! Enough! If Celeste hadn't sued the NIAR through my law firm," Odom snarled, "we all know that Sslits would have been a splatter on a Petri dish somewhere years ago. If you think anything has c-changed in our c-c-commitment..."

His voice beginning to shake, Odom stopped, clenching and unclenching his fists to calm himself before he continued.

"If you hassle us one more time..."

Wood raised his hand and stopped Odom.

"I know, I know. I'll be the splatter," Wood said, finishing the lawyer's sentence for him. "Big words from a very little man."

"You'll never get away with this!" said Odom.

"So, sue me..." said Wood as he waved his contingent of men away. "Again."

Both Odom and Celeste stood for several long moments, watching Wood and his men leave, before speaking to one another.

The conversation was terse and all of it belonged to Odom.

"You couldn't have handled Wood any worse than you did. You may be a highly educated scientist, Celeste, but you don't know the first thing about how to handle people. Frankly, sometimes you not only amaze me with your clumsiness in human relationships, you disgust me as well."

"Wow," answered Gaines, "you really are in love of me, Larry."

"Oh, God, Celeste. You are an idiot."

Celeste started to respond, but Odom's raised hand, palm forward, stopped her.

CHAPTER TWENTY FOUR

The afternoon traffic was light on 5th Street heading East through downtown Tulsa when an olive green 1993 Chevy Blazer accelerated out from behind a white 1995 Ford Cargo Van and quickly sped ahead of it. The roar of the Blazer engine was joined by the sound of the blaring horns of two other vehicles in the left lane, swerving partially onto the adjacent sidewalk to miss it. The handful of Tulsans on that sidewalk scattered like discarded scraps of newspaper towards or into the entrances of the skyscrapers that soared up on either side of the street.

With the squeal of the Blazer's tires that echoed in the man-made canyon, the Chevy jerked right, out of the left lane thirty yards in front of the Ford, and screeched to a dead stop diagonally across the lane.

Trying to miss the two ton promise of death, the driver of the Ford Van slammed on his brakes, leaving skid marks on the road and bringing his vehicle to an askance stop just three feet short from the side of the Blazer.

The sign painted in cerulean blue on both sides of the Cargo Van read *Airship Advertising The Sky is the Limit!*

Almost simultaneously, the driver of the Ford threw his door open and jumped out onto the street as five uniformed men disgorged from the Blazer.

The driver of the Ford yelled, "What is goin'…" but his words died on his lips.

He stopped cold, swallowed hard, and raised his arms at the sight of the drawn side-arms of three of the men in green, military uniforms and the machineguns resting in the crooks of the arms of the remaining two soldiers, all trotting towards him.

One of those soldiers yelled, "Bomb threat!! Move away from the van! Now!!"

The director for *Airship Advertising* stepped sheepishly away from the vehicle as the four other men in green, on reaching the Ford Cargo Van, wrenched open its side doors and pulled two terrified and confused men and one woman out onto the street.

As they did so, the rubbernecking driver of a yellow, well-used 1987 Volkswagen in the left lane was violently waved on by the barrel of one of the machineguns.

What appeared to be the commanding officer of the operation stopped two feet in front of the advertising director of *Airship Advertising* as two of the soldiers trotted to the back of the van and wrenched its doors open. They leapt inside.

The director said, "We were only shooting a commercial..." to the sound of the inside of his van being trashed.

The soldier barked, "I don't give a bloody damn what you were doing. This is a matter of National Security. You will stand down, and, after we are done, go on your way as if nothing ever happened. Do...you...understand."

It was not a question.

The director nodded his head.

Suddenly, a flurry of film and a camera that had been wrecked exploded out of the back of the van. The film pooled out of the camera like writhing, black snakes onto the street.

The director choked, "my commercial..?"

TUESDAY, NOVEMBER 26TH, 1996
SECLUDED WOOD NORTH OF TULSA OKLAHOMA

As the buckle of the Bible belt in mid-western America, Tulsa was and is no stranger to midnight baptisms, sometimes as the normal expression of a profound love and commitment, and sometimes in ugly, odd places and under even uglier circumstances. But the dark sky of late Tuesday night hid a profound perversion in a decidedly alien fount; a profane mockery of both the blood of Christ and outré K'huprician ritual.

What was a monstrous Other in the eyes of man, Spashs, was now to become an abomination on two planets, divided from human beings by much more than just immense physical distance.

It was not the first time.

What was separate was now becoming an empathic melding of alien and human memory:

of elephant headed gods and sacred cows, and multiple blood-red suns hung high above cracked K'huprician desert; of dirty government clinics on the streets of Delhi, and the vast, frozen emptiness of space and time twisted beyond human understanding; undying hatred on a leprous, mangled face, and of the instinctive fury of a horror without a face.

And above all, of the Hive.

Tonight, alien and human would become one in an ungodly coupling.

An unhuman coupling...past shame.

The excitement for leprous Firoz Babur wasn't as powerful as it had been so many years ago in India, the expectation of new physical vigor, of the end of shame, of the reversal of the slow corruption of his unclean mind and his unclean skin and his unclean hair and his unclean internal organs. He knew it would come, the nonsexual orgasm, the sensual, electric thrill racing down his extremities and up again that some feel at the beating of a huge, struck, temple gong, or the sight of teeming, surging life on a congested Indian street, or at the washing away of sin and disease in the Ganges. But familiarity had diminished the thrill a jot.

That diminished ecstasy ran down his legs and up his arms as, carefully, slowly, reverently, Firoz lay back and began to sink onto the alien concave bed deep in the guts of the flying saucer and into the alien horror that lay on it beneath him.

Like almonds dropped in honey, he thought; a stupid thought, but his nevertheless.

Firoz closed his eyes and inhaled deeply before he sank completely inside Spashs.

Totally immersed in the alien, the years of unrelenting poverty and anguish grew hazy in his mind as leprosy began to melt away from his feet and his hands. His ingested nose and ear and the three fingers on his left hand began to regenerate into healthy pink flesh.

He thought *Wet. Glistening with life. Reborn. Rejuvenated. New.*

What limp strands of his hair that had been left hanging from his otherwise scarred, bald skull began to grow back in tight curls and Firoz's upper lip that had rotted away once again covered his top row of teeth.

Firoz's initial terror of drowning during his first rebirth never even entered his mind as Pariah's lungs filled once more and his gag reflex sucked in ever greater dollops of Spashs' goop into his lungs. He inhaled Spashs deeply into his lungs, and the angry red nodules that had checker-boarded an otherwise fish-belly white face and deadened his skin faded.

Then for moments that crawled by like centuries, and as Pariah metamorphosed, his mind exploded like a blown dandelion into pinpoints of light and he hallucinated.

He found himself not enveloped in alien mucous, nor lying prone in a flying saucer, or even on Earth Seven, but floating in a cloudless, pale green sky thousands of feet above an unending alien landscape scorched by three enormous blood red suns. The greatest of the searing suns on the horizon was the size of his head, the least the size of his thumb.

Immense fields of what he somehow knew was a brownish mold as fragile as peanut brittle were random splotches on the desert. Like the manna sent by God to Moses and the Israelites, this was what fed the horrors of K'hupric.

He knew this was Sslits' planet. This was Spashs' planet. This was K'hupric.

It was a parched planet that swarmed beneath the sand in an endless tangle of tunnels with countless squirming placenta bags of mucous, as yet unseen but nevertheless sensed.

Firoz continued to sink lower and lower and lower to its pimpled surface. He knew these putrid horrors were called Sslits, and that he was floating above a planet that was no more than a blister on a cosmic furnace, a world of nothing but cracked earth; no plants, no insects, no oceans or streams or ponds or puddles, never clouds heavy with rain.

Then Spashs belched and sloshed within its skin of hard water.

In a fetal ball, Pariah twisted inside the alien on Earth Seven as he also floated only dozens of feet above a massive mound of yellow, cracked earth, an alien anthill in the otherwise deserted, exhausted desert.

Like a ghost, feet first, Pariah sank into a side of the mound.

He remembered that, even before he had sunk into the massive cavern inside the mound city of K'hupric, a sacred liquid trickle there into a stone basin that was an alien altar, and that, once a torrent, each liquid drop was now utterly priceless because water was life and almost none existed on K'hupric outside of what was treasured and stored in each gelatinous body of each K'huprician. He knew because Spashs knew.

Spashs hiccupped and Pariah fell out of the ceiling of the cavern and above that basin.

" FIROZ CONTINUED TO SINK LOWER ... "

As he floated there, two monstrous K'huprician priests lumbered into the chamber in their natural, putrid, hideous forms, one carrying a glob of wailing mucous that Pariah sensed was a child that would be baptized in that altar.

In Pariah's head, Spashs said, *Wails of new HIVE rises.*

Pariah impossibly glanced up through the ceiling of the cavern into the K'huprician sky as one silver flying saucer soundlessly rose and diminished in size into the green atmosphere, and a look of sudden understanding transfigured his face.

He knew the ship roaring into space was in search of a new world, ripe for invasion. He knew that time as he understood it had become twisted and he was witnessing a launch decades in the past. He knew because Spashs knew.

Pariah looked down as the wailing amorphous infant was lowered into the thin skin of water in the basin.

In Firoz's head, Spashs said, *No waters for new hive.*
No waters sslits dies.

Pariah squirmed inside Spashs.

In Pariah's head, Spashs said, *NO ships return no new worlds for new hive.*

What had been murky those many years ago had been clear and sharp to the leper for at least the last ten years of his life when communication with the alien had finally become possible. So he had long known that a judge and executioner named Spashs had been sent to track down the missing scout ship because to fail a mission and live is treason against the Hive. Sslits—the pilot of that ship—had committed treason, the ultimate betrayal on K'hupric.

And Pariah knew he meant to be the instrument of brutal punishment; the punishment was death.

Pariah, his head slightly downturned, opened his eyes.

He thought *now I know what Spashs and Sslits know!! And Sslits can no longer hide.*

Inside Firoz's head, Spashs said, *Yeesssss! Death for Sslits. Death for Sslits parasites Celestes.*

Pariah asked, "But doesn't Sslits also know where we are ...?"

NO! Spashs blocks Sslits.

Then the altar and the cavern and the yellow desert and the three suns fell apart like a blown dandelion and the Indian named Firoz and called Pariah sat up, trailing long lines of alien spittle from himself to the alien, his body still glistening from the mucous still covering him.

He inhaled deeply, and said, "I have the body you need to move among men and lure the traitor to Spashs."

Yes to kill!

Pariah sat, the lower part of his body still partially immersed in the alien, and closed his eyes again, his face and body healed and young again, smiling; his torso, arms and head glistened from the rancid alien mucous that, moments ago, had covered his entire body.

Then Spashs rose up and poured out of the concave chair, looking with eyes with dead, mock pupils at Pariah, watching Pariah's lungs rhythmically rise and fall, rise and fall, rise and fall as the Indian shook off his profoundly deep hallucinogenic sleep.

CHAPTER TWENTY FIVE

Pariah hopped off of the slimy concave alien bed, looking no older than twenty-five years of age, so full of joy that he was oblivious of the bed or Spashs or of the room or anything else. He stood motionless but as euphoric as someone high on drugs, and opened his eyes.

He asked, "But, how...?! Spashs has said that I failed when I thought I had killed Slits?"

One of its four tentacles of slime imitating a human arm and hand sprouted out of Spashs gob to point behind the Indian.

SEE

A small section of the wall behind Pariah slid up revealing a niche. In the niche sat a huge, silver twist of licorice, a cylinder four feet long and a foot in circumference that seemed made of long silver strands of metal twisted like a huge stick of licorice.

Spashs pointing tentacle of slime came to rest on Firoz' shoulder.

Instantly, an explosion of light filled the Indian's inner eye, and he watched a K'huprician walk to a table on which stood a twisted silver cylinder.

It patted the top of the silver licorice three times.

An incredibly intense, soundless, searing beam of colorless light discharged out of the opening at its tip.

The wall facing it exploded with tornadic force, disintegrating into red hot dust and shards of debris.

Then the vision fell apart like spent fireworks and Spashs withdrew its temporary appendage and said, *What Ssslits' knows Spashs knows Pariah knows. Now pariahs go Spashs go. Now Spashs kill.*

With the pleasure of epiphany, Pariah smiled and said, "*Yes.*"

TUESDAY, NOV. 26TH, 1996
TULSA, NEAR DOWNTOWN IN THE GREENWOOD WAREHOUSE
DISTRICT

The psychic barrier was shattered. Sslits jerked up into a sitting position on its makeshift bed of mattresses.

Spashs was in its cellular mind.

Sslits swelled up to a standing position. It moved sluggishly to the only window in its room in the Tribune building.

It prepared itself for the city/mound beneath the blazing three red suns, for the sled, for the ceremonial feasting.

It prepared itself for death.

•••

The pastels of dusk settled over the almost deserted buildings, many of them Art Deco skyscrapers, and empty streets of a downtown Tulsa that had once teemed, night and day and for decades, with businessmen, shop keepers, shoppers, the office workers of petroleum and insurance companies, the ad men and women in advertising agencies, and city, state and federal workers. Framed by the streets running east and west, and looking like a painting, the sun had half-sunk beneath the horizon beyond the Arkansas River leaving layers of sherbet colored clouds in the sky.

The few retail shops and little weekday, hole-in-the-wall restaurants that still opened downtown closed their doors each day as the offices and businesses emptied out, just before the sun set, and did not open on weekends. A few bums lay like crumpled piles of rags in doorways here and there, mostly asleep or in drunken stupors.

The muffled hum of distant traffic, the click of stop signals that continued to blink in the early evening through their sequence of red, yellow and green, flurries of birds that rose and set, rose and set from the ledges of the skyscrapers, or the great whir of the brushes of a street cleaning truck were its only sounds.

Tulsans who had worked downtown had created the suburbs even as they had fled the skyscrapers and business offices and churches and congested streets for a less cramped lifestyle. Now the only movement in the empty streets was newspapers and discarded scraps of paper that danced when caught up by a stray breeze.

The old cliché of shooting a cannon and hitting no one was almost true; occasionally, some thug or societal outcast who ran astray of the crooks, gang members, and low-life that infest every city did end their lives there, however, at the end of a gun barrel.

Only a few salesmen and an odd assortment of relatives visiting their big city families were left in the great and small hotels downtown.

All was business as usual but for one exception at the almost forgotten Tribune newspaper building on Archer Street, the southwest edge of the almost always deserted Brady warehouse district. Built in 1924 when Tulsa was home to multiple newspapers, the six-story, red brick building had stood mostly empty for decades as Tulsa continued to grow to the south.

The Brady district was almost always empty except for the occasional entertainment at the huge Brady Theater and the once famous home of Country Swing, Cain's Ballroom.

That exception was the red slime, pencil thin beginning to ooze out of the casing, grilles, and sash of one of the large Sunburst windows on the bottom floor on the East side of the building. That ooze looked like a red cake frosting squeezed out of a piping bag. The entire interior surface of the window was obscured on the inside with the disgusting mucous. Its panes of glass, slightly bulging from the pressure behind, were outlined with red, gloppy squares and rectangles, each bordering the other.

It was the only window of the bed room to which Sslits was restricted.

The red ooze puckered as it expanded into red veins that eventually burst and sent rivulets of goop crawling down the window to slowly drip onto the street below as the room behind it seemed to empty of the stuff, bleeding out. That slow crawl because a pool beneath the window that grew into a gelatinous mound that rose up and up and up and became Sslits.

The alien looked somewhat like Jimi Hendrix with back-blown spiked hair.

CHAPTER TWENTY SIX

The window, the man, and the building sat opposite the Tribune newspaper building.

The unshaven man who sat in the dark behind a second story window in that building on a folding chair startled.

His cigarette fell out of his mouth

He dropped his binoculars.

He knew what it was supposed to look like. He had seen the classified photographs. And he was, after all, a professional. He had prepared himself mentally. But his dispassionate suspension of disbelief was shattered by what he watched lumbering east down a short stretch of Archer Street towards Main Street.

He snatched up his binoculars with shaking hands and looked again.

He whispered, "Holy Mother of God" and snatched up the Walkie-talkie with his right hand that sat on a second folding chair on his right side. He talked while still holding the binoculars over his eyes with his left hand.

"This is 040 reporting. This is 040 calling. For God's sake, pick up. Pick up!! It's heading into the Brady district," the agent hissed. "You need to get the team down here, right now, sir...what?!?"

He listened to the voice on the other end of the Walkie-talkie.

He answered, "Well, it ain't goin' out for pizza!"

He listened to the voice on the other end of the line.

"Yes, sir, I'm sorry. Yes, sir, not again. It's just about at Main Street. Now it's turning North down Main Street headed for Brady Street."

The voice on the other end of the Walkie-talkie said something.

"You're damn right I won't get near it. Yes, sir."

The voice on the other end of the line went dead. The unshaven man sat for several moments with the Walkie-talkie still held by his ear before he slowly lowered it to his side.

He placed the binoculars firmly over both eyes again and scanned the area below him.

The monster from Hell that had forever changed his concept of reality was gone.

•••

Talking around the expensive cigar in his mouth, Toren Walker said, "Thank you. Relay the message back to 040."

Walker placed the telephone back in its cradle next to a Tiffany lamp that sat on a mahogany end table. It rested next to one of two, black, leather chairs were he sat in a luxury suite in the Doubletree Hotel in downtown Tulsa about a half mile away from the Tribune building. He was wearing a pair of creased, black slacks with a starched white shirt, its long sleeves rolled up to his elbows.

Dressed in civilian clothes, Charles Wood was sitting in the other chair, nursing a half-empty glass of bourbon.

The former Lt. General was holding his own glass of bourbon, straight, in his left hand. It was full for the second time. The lamp threw a cone of hazy, yellow light around him in the otherwise dark room. Its weak light did nothing to obscure the look of subtle joy on Walker's flat, hardened face.

He took the cigar out of his mouth and laid it, still smoking, in the ash tray on the end table. Walker whispered, "finally' in a small voice not intended to be heard by anyone but himself despite the fact that Wood sat, somewhat subdued, immediately across from him. As he said it, he felt as if he were the Christ in His last moments on the cross.

He chuckled.

He took a sip of the bourbon.

Then Toren said, "Everything is in place. Get out the limo, Jeeves. It's time."

Wood shook his head, disappointed.

"Are you sure you want me to do this now?"

Dispassionately, Toren said, "Look at me. I should have done this twenty years ago, but I couldn't get all the dominos in a row. What opportunity did I have earlier to separate that inaccessible alien slime ball from Celeste long enough to pull this off? Until a few days ago, she and it had never been out of the compound in Roswell!

"The doctors tell me I don't have long to live. My body is just worn out, Charles. Of course it's time. Are you turning yellow on me at the last minute?"

"Of course not. You know me better than that."

"She is the only living thing on Earth that seems to have any control over Sslits. If we can get her to command that thing to make me young again instead of killing me…to make me young again, Charles!!"

"Well, Toren, I'm almost certain that will happen, although it might take a little longer than you think it will."

"And if we can get Celeste and Sslits to our little prearranged hideout where I can have my shot at continuing to live without half of Tulsa knowing about it..."

"That's quite a few ifs, Toren. I can't guarantee it; hell, I can't guarantee anything in life. But I think it can all fall into place."

"And the biggest if of all. If I can get that thing to let me take a little bath in it..."

Wood interrupted. "That's quite a long shot in and of itself."

Toren picked up his cigar from the ash tray, poked it back in his mouth, and leaned forward in his chair. He took the cigar out and blew a smoke ring into the air. He poked it back in. There was a wild fire in his old eyes that surprised Wood somewhat; it wasn't typical for the man who had played such a major part in his life.

"All the ifs have to happen, Charles. We have to make them happen. Taking a dip in that alien thing is the only hope I have left.

"If, if, if.

"If I don't, I die."

CHAPTER TWENTY SEVEN

The torn scrap of newspaper floated down to the sidewalk to join several other scraps.

Dusk was slowly settling into early evening and painting shadows on everything as Sslits stood on the northeast corner of Archer and Main, tearing little strips off of the discarded newspaper he had snatched up from the sidewalk. Its pupil-less eyes watched the scrap as it fluttered down with the awe on its pseudo-face of a newborn baby experiencing something for the first time.

The unshaven man who had been told to follow the creature at a safe distance was watching from behind the corner of a building about thirty feet away. He carried the same Walkie-talkie at his hip in his right hand that he had used to report the alien's appearance on the street. Fear, excitement and expectancy passed rapidly over his face.

Sslits tore off another scrap of paper, but did not watch its descent. The alien dropped the newspaper as well, having lost interest, and lumbered on up on the east side of Main Street that rose on a slight incline. As it did so, a sign several blocks away and atop an old story-and-a-half tall building lit up. The neon sign was raised on a metal supports high above the building's forty-five degree angled roof. Its yellow letters read: Cain's.

Above the sign, the air shimmered from the heat of the fading day.

Sslits stopped.

The alien raised its right pseudo-fist up to its imitation mouth and bit one of the knuckles on its three-fingered hand. It had seen an excited human child do so on one of the countless television shows it had watched for decades at Roswell.

Its eye fully on the sign, Sslit began to slosh up the slightly inclined sidewalk towards the new revelation three blocks away. The Cain's sign grew larger with each step.

Sslits said, ?Won't yous come out tonight?

When the alien saw the bum slumped in the doorway of the empty warehouse just north of Brady Street, it stopped again.

The bum reclined in a complete, drunken stupor, leaning half-upright against the doorjamb, in the doorway under a blanket of newspapers. Only his head was visible. His eyes were closed, but he still clutched a half empty wine bottle in his dirty left hand that also rested on the sidewalk. He was snoring.

Sslits began to shake, clutching and unclenching its hands.

The unshaven spy leaned a little further out from the edge of the building.

The K'huprician's quasi-human face, distorted with rage, its mouth disjointed, its eyes burning, and screaming in silent fury, took a step forward and snatched the drunk in a shower of falling newspaper up from the sidewalk and out of the doorway.

The wino startled and woke up.

Sslits raised the bum up, face up to its hideous face now all teeth and mouth and fire.

Horror dilated the bum's rummy eyes. He opened his toothless mouth to scream.

The scream was cut short…as Sslits tore his head off and dropped it on the sidewalk.

Thirty feet or so behind Sslits, looking around the corner of a building, the unshaven man's face drained of blood. He turned from his hiding place and vomited against the wall of the building that hid him from the alien.

•••

At that moment, a black van rolled quietly to a stop on Archer Street across from the Tribune building and behind an older sedan already parked there.

In that sedan, a man picked up a large mobile phone from where it lay next to him on the bench seat and dialed Eric Gaines.

He said, "Sslits has left the Tribune."

He turned off the phone, turned the ignition key, and pulled the sedan onto Archer, headed west.

The alien dropped the drunk's headless body, having lost interest, and lumbered on up Main Street.

The spy, his stomach empty, dropped his Walkie-Talkie, turned, and ran away.

On Archer across from the Tribune, the doors of the black van opened.

•••

Sslits stood before Cain's, looking up at a smaller sign in an inverted L that jutted horizontally from the front of the building. Although the alien could not read, the sign read: Cain's (in the vertical leg of the L) Ballroom Dancing. Below that sign, barred windows flanking both sides of a large door that was the main entrance were inset into natural stone.

Sslits lunged forward and pressed its body against the stone on the right side of the entrance, and it doing so, flattened itself into a spreading thick goo as its human appearance dissipated. That alien mucous began to crawl up the wall, seemingly defying gravity, slowly passing the height of the entrance, up until it reached the slight overhang of the roof, up and over that overhang and onto the roof. Reaching the roof, it began to regenerate, first, into a mound of quivering jelly, then into a large stump of coagulating goop, growing legs, and arms, and a head with a sheath of back-blown spiked hair, and finally a mouth, nose, and pupil-less eyes.

Sslits straddled the apex of the roof, absorbing the visual banquet below and to its south that was downtown Tulsa.

It gurgled, Celestes.

Sslits sat across the peak of the roof, on the ghost of its K'huprician city/mound, under the phantom of three blazing hot suns, waiting to die.

It looked somewhat like Shirley Temple.

CHAPTER TWENTY EIGHT

O dom plopped down into the second of the two folding chairs in Celeste's hideaway in the abandoned Tribune building as if he were dead weight. There were big half-moon stains on his suit under each underarm, and his usually meticulous hair was matted.

As far as Celeste was concerned, he was just that tonight, dead weight.

She finished rummaging through her clothing in one of the two pieces of luggage she'd brought with her that were stacked against the wall of the room, removing her journal. Weary, strung out, and defeated, she then sat down in the remaining chair and opened the journal. The first line she read was:

In the dead of night, the living dead...

She thought *well at least that's appropriate.*

That line, that fragment of a sentence, in her journal, one of more than forty journals that she had filled with her most private thoughts since that fateful day in 1947, seemed silly to her now, melodramatic, even for the naïve woman that she had been when she originally wrote it.

In hindsight, that idealistic woman seemed even more ridiculous as Celeste looked around the dusty, dark, barren room where she sat on a cheap metal folding chair. She was reading her journal by the weak light thrown off of one of the propane lamps in the room, this one sitting on top of the box it had come in; her suitcase that had held her journal was open and shoved up against the bare wall in shadows; her sleeping bag was rolled up like a log next to it.

Odom was rolled up like a log in the chair were he sat, struggling to keep his eyes open.

She thought *what has all of this gotten me.*

She read on.

I am almost certain that the creatures on Sslits's planet communicate telepathically, each of them linked to the other almost like ants seem linked together. It is also probable that the enormous distance between the K'huprician planet and Sslits stranded on Earth had certainly severed that telepathic link forty-eight years ago when Sslits was shipwrecked here.

That separateness from Hive certainly must have driven the alien near madness.

I am firmly convinced that that silence was what drove Sslits to link somehow with me, although not telepathically.

Celeste stopped reading for a moment, then flipped through pages until she came to the first of a series of clean sheets. She began to write.

When I was a young girl and still reading science fiction books, I read an interview with an SF writer. In answer to a question I found fascinating, he said something I've never forgotten.

The question was, 'why do aliens always look like insects, or octopodidae, or birds, or lizards'. He answered, 'Because if they were completely and truly alien and we human beings had no point of context, we wouldn't even be able to recognize them as living, possibly even sentient, creatures.

She stopped writing and turned to face her lawyer as Odom said, "I've had it with you and that alien pus bag and the Mall and the shopping center and the twenty years of nonsense I've put up with to date. I'm wrung out. I'm dead tired. So I'm going back to my third rate hotel room, mix myself a stiff Grasshopper, sprawl out of my couch, smoke a pack of cigarettes, and try to fall asleep watching some tepid TV movie.

"Don't call me. Don't drop by. Don't even think about me."

She waved him away, and returned to her journal.

I must not be half as smart as I thought I was, because it took me a damn long time to learn—or admit—that that science fiction writer was right. As for its physical being, if Sslits didn't look like a placenta sack of red maggots, he— it would have never even been found in that saucer.

I'm finally ready to admit it now. Why?

Because I am a failure, a complete fool who submersed her life to the total belief that every mystery or puzzle or question has an answer and that the methodical application of scientific principals can find any and all answers. That I was smart enough to know any thing and everything.

But my total belief in science didn't solve the problems of my disastrous marriage. It didn't stop Eric from getting custody of my two children. It didn't teach me how to have healthy relationships with my colleagues, or my superiors in the scientific community, or even how to handle the media.

Stripped to the bone, the real truth is that I don't know what I'm doing. There is no precedent to follow. I have been one of the scientists, the principal scientist, to discover a new species of animal not of this planet that wasn't created by or isn't subject to the physical laws of Earth.

I have spent decades—most of my adult life—in trying to unravel the mystery of Sslits because I really thought I could add something to our general knowledge of the universe when, the truth be known, I really thought it would make me a superstar in my field. Those decades in Roswell, however, became nothing but a prison.

And after decades of the most intensive scientific enquiry that I can imagine, I know only two facts about Sslits with certainty, that it shares the instinct for survival will all other living creatures, and that it fears pain and loves pleasure.

Everything else I know is supposition.

Whoopee do.

Celeste glanced over at Odom. His head resting on his chest, the lawyer was fast asleep in his folding chair. She returned to her journal.

If this thing from the stars is even sentient, do its thought processes parallel human thought?

I have no certain knowledge of whether Sslits was the cook or the Captain of the flying saucer that crashed in New Mexico. Its responses to the hundreds of organic and non-organic objects I exposed to it for decades was so random, so devoid of any understanding of cause and effect on Earth Seven, that I have no way to measure those responses against anything human. Does it even understand a word I've ever said? It would seem so, but the snatches of song lyrics it parrots in response to anything and everything said by anyone implies otherwise.

I am so tired now. I'm not certain that I can go on anymore. I see no light at the end of the tunnel for me or for it. When Larry finds out about the Brady fiasco, I'll have no defense to stand on. He will hang me out to dry just like everyone else. I know only one thing with certainly now.

I am a failure.

No. I know and finally admit another; Sslits cannot be assimilated into human society.

Because of its random, horrific violence...

Sslits must be destroyed.

Celeste looked up from her journal. Odom was snoring, fast asleep in his folding chair, his head still resting on his chest.

A whimsical smile on her face, she barked, "Odom! Wake up!!"

He woke up with a start.

"You fell asleep. You are exhausted. Get up and go to your hotel."

Odom struggled up from his folding chair.

He said, "That's one hell of a way to wake up a lawyer. I was just beating Perry Mason for the first time in court when you yelled."

"Yeah, yeah, yeah. Check on Sslits before you go, will yah, to see if he's still in semi-hibernation."

As the lawyer walked to the door of Sslit's room, stepping around the ice chest next to it on the floor, Odom said, "Yeah, yeah, yeah yourself."

He opened the door. He looked in. He looked again.

He said, "What th' hell…"

Then the door to Celeste's room slammed open.

●●●

At that moment, outside of the Tribune building, a dirty black van slowly crawled to a stop on the opposite side of Archer Street. Its headlights were off. The door of the driver's side swung slowly and quietly open.

Firoz Babur stepped out.

Then leaning back into the van, he picked up something from the bench seat next to the steering wheel. He closed the door carefully, making as little noise as possible.

Pariah straightened up. He held a queer bazooka in his hands.

As he did so, the other three doors of the van opened slowly and quietly as well. A woman stepped out of the passenger's side of the van. Instead of wearing the sexy clothing by which she had hoped to seduce Sslits, she now wore a nondescript blouse and pants, and a bulky flame thrower.

One after the other, two additional men exited the back passenger doors, closing the doors quietly behind them. One dressed in a cowboy hat, shirt, jeans and boots, carried a Thompson machine gun. Four hand grenades hung from a leather belt around the trim waist of the second man.

All four of them met at the front of the van.

Leaning forward and slightly bent at the waist as if he shared a secret in a whisper, Firoz hissed, "You each know what to do. Do it well, and we all live the life of Riley after tonight. Do it wrong, and we all die like rats. You two," Parish continued, indicating the two other men with a wave of his hand, "Stay Close."

Then leaning intimately close to the woman and laying a hand on her shoulder, he said, "You too, sweetheart."

Lisa Ferry nodded.

CHAPTER TWENTY NINE

Odom opened the door to Sslits room. He looked in. He looked again.
He said, "What th' hell…"

And then the door to Celeste's room exploded in and struck the wall to its left. It rebounded, swinging partially closed only to be stopped by a black, booted foot.

Charles Wood stood in the doorway, out of his uniform, his hand gun drawn.

Close behind him stood two other men in plain clothes, also with their revolvers drawn. The man on Wood's right side had a length of rope hanging from his left wrist. The man at his left side chewed something in his mouth that made his left cheek bulge.

For a second, Odom and Celeste froze. Then Celeste's started to raise her right hand to the lapel of her white robe.

"Drop it!!" Wood demanded, his voice as hard and cold as ice, his eyes dead.

Celeste let her hand drop.

Her voice dead, she said, "What the hell are you doing, Charley."

Wood snapped, "Shut up."

He waved the man on his right side forward with his gun.

"Jake, take care of her idiot lawyer. Steve, stay close."

Steve nodded yes and spat a wad of chewing tobacco on the floor by his feet.

Odom watched as Wood approached the lawyer, his mind racing among the options open to him, his eyes never leaving the gun.

Celeste said, "He's bluffing, Larry, or they would have just shot us when they first walked in."

Wood's eyes narrowed as he snarled, "I…said…shut up!"

Odom saw Jake begin to lower the gun. He lunged to his left, and, snatching up the propane lamp on the floor, threw it with all of his strength at Wood's gunman.

Celeste leapt up from her chair, her forgotten journal falling to the floor.
She lunged at Wood and the second agent.

The lamp missed its mark and smashed to the floor but did not shatter.

Wood raised his hand gun and fired it once into the ceiling. The second agent, Steve, tackled Celeste in midair as Wood stepped back and to one side of her.

Larry Odom stepped back only to hit the wall behind him. In an instant, Jake raised his arm and punched Odom in the face with the barrel of his gun.

Odom moaned, hit the wall with the back of his head, and slumped.

As Celeste plunged to his right side with both of Steve's arms around her waist, Wood swung his right arm up and down hard on the back of her neck.

Celeste and Steve tumbled to the floor.

Bleeding just below his right eye, Odom saw nothing as Jake raised his arm high and brought the butt on his gun down hard against the lawyer's right temple.

Odom fell to the floor, unconscious, striking and overturning the ice cooler. Its latch broken, its lid sprang open and the ice and canned soda pop inside was hurled out to fan across the floor towards Celeste.

Huffing and cursing under her breath, Celeste struggled with all of her strength to pull away from the man on top of her, but Steve was too strong and heavy.

Wood took a step towards both of their bodies thrashing on the floor, swung his left leg back, and kicked Celeste in the ribs.

She exhaled and lay still.

Wood barked, "Get her back up in the chair, Steve, and tie her damn hands behind her back."

Leaving Odom on the floor, Jake joined Steve to lift Celeste up by the armpits, her head slumped on her chest, and drug her to the folding chair. Using the rope tied around his wrist, Wood's flunkies tied Celeste's hands together behind the chair.

Wood said, "Check the second room, Jake, just to be sure."

Then he squatted by Celeste, leering. He said, "Well, I've got to give you some credit. You fought like a wildcat against old Steve, there, and Steve's a former semi-pro wrestler."

As he spoke, he disconnected the microphone from the inside of her lapel from the cable leading to the transmitter/receiver that was tapped under her robe over her ribs.

He said, "Let's save this little electronic jewel for a bit later, shall we, honey?"

" CHECK THE SECOND ROOM, JAKE ... "

Celeste said nothing.

"Your lapdog must have been surprised when he saw Sslits gone," sneered Wood. "Not us. My plant across the street saw your bag of snot seep through a window and head north up Main Street a good ten minutes ago. I'm guessing a couple of minutes more and lover boy'll arrive back. No reason we can't get to know one another until showtime."

Jake reappeared in the doorway to Sslit's room, indicating a positive on it being empty by lifting a thumb up.

Charles grinned. "Just like I said."

Celeste raised her head and said, "You're a liar."

Wood slapped her across the cheek, just enough to sting.

He snarled, "Is that so. Go ahead, call him. This isn't a game this time."

Celeste yelled, "Sslits!!"

Wood chuckled.

Celeste yelled, "Sslits!!" again, only louder.

Wood chuckled.

Celeste said, "You've sunk to a new low this time. I must admit, I didn't even think that was possible. You didn't have to do that to Larry."

"Oh, but it was such fun."

"Why are you doing this? Have you finally lost your mind? You can't arrest me; you have no authority to do that. Are you going to kill me? Did Toren send you to kill me? Are you going to rape me? Rape me and then kill me? This is insanity. Sslits will tear you to shreds."

Gloating, Wood stretched to his full height, inflated his cheeks, and then exhaled.

"You're bein' coy, aren't 'cha, baby? You know and I know…'cause we both have one."

"What the hell are you talking about?"

"Your master talks in your head," said Wood, ignoring her statement. "And does things to your body. Nice things. Mine…well, mine thinks that I'm his little boot lick, but Toren's got a painful surprise coming to him, and very, very soon."

Bending at the waist, he placed his left hand on the arm of Celeste's chair while still holding his hand gun in his right hand and leaned intimately close to her face. Before she turned her face away and to her left side where Steve stood, she saw a wild fire in Wood's eyes.

"I got a painful surprise myself just a couple of months ago that changed everything. And it's going to change everything about our relationship, you and me, honey."

Celeste said, "Get away from me."

Wood said, "I'm dying."

"What?"

"I said, I'm dying, you cheap slut. And that's why I'm here, and that's why I'm doing this, and that's why I'm going to do what I'm going to do."

"You're a liar."

"You don't believe me? If you don't have an open mind, I could give you one," continued Wood, "I could give you a nice big hole."

He placed the muzzle of his gun against Celeste's temple.

"But that would mess up my carefully laid plans, sweetheart. The doctors say I have an inoperable brain tumor, and I have one or two months left, at best. So, I'm going to use that time the best way I know how.

"Here's how it's going down. In a moment or two, I'm going to reattach your microphone and you're going to call Sslits back here. Your voice will sound urgent because this business is urgent and more. And when that bag of snot gets here, you are going to tell it to do to me what it did to you to make you young and healthy."

Wood straightened.

Celeste snorted. "Like Hell I will. What's to stop me from telling Sslit to tear you apart?"

Wood patted his left pants pocket.

"I've got a little concussion grenade in this pocket that says he won't be touching me, Celeste. Jake and Steve have them to. So, unless you want Lawyer Larry and Sslits blown to bits, you'll make sure that doesn't happen."

"Grenades would kill all of us, Charley."

"I'm already a dead man, honey. And if you don't call that alien thing back, honey pot, my man Jake there is going to start by blowing Larry Odom's brains out all over the wall behind him with his little pop gun. Now, do you really want to clean up a mess like that?"

Celeste said, "Bite me."

Wood slapped her hard on the cheek with the back of his hand.

Then he leaned in close again, raising his left hand to the lapel of her robe.

"Now, let's just recon…" and as he said it, he kissed her on the mouth.

With enough power to make her own chair rock back on its legs, and lifting him an inch off of the floor, Celeste kicked him in the crotch.

As she did so, she snarled, "Kiss…this!!!"

Wood exhaled breath and collapsed hard on the floor sideways, dropping his handgun, and clutching his crotch with both hands.

In the blink of an eye, Jake knelt at Wood's side to lift him, moaning and rolling back and forth, off the floor when the thug froze there, his eyes wide with confusion and terror at what stood in the doorway to the room.

He said, "Mother of God."

At that same moment, Steve, who had been watching the door, saw it as well. He swung his hand gun away from Celeste and pointed it at the horror there.

Its sham-human head rose in a gelatinous tiara of mucous above a mockery of dead human eyes, and its tongue hung from a bear-trap of needle sharp, gnashing teeth. Its four arms ending in claws writhed like snakes from a torso covered with blisters of tiny, bleached, human skulls. Grey cobra shaped welts circled its ankles and wrists, and a skirt of pseudo-human arms and hands hung like a skirt around its faux hips.

With its two lowest arms, it held a giant stick of silver licorice across its forearms.

The silver twist hummed with a crescendo of power.

Steve said, "Damn!" and swallowed his wad of chewing tobacco.

Celeste cried out, "Sslits!!" although she knew it was hopeless to do so.

In that doorway, Spashs hissed, *CELESTES.*

CHAPTER THIRTY

Sslits straddled the apex of the roof of Cain's Ballroom just below its sign, three blocks away from the Tribune. Its Shirley Temple face and its pupil-less eyes were turned up to the heavens and the visual banquet of the night sky; the glutted, just rising yellow moon and the unimaginably distant planets that were merely larger specks among the countless stars.

Sslits said, Gosh.

On its home planet, twilight was as brilliant with light because of its suns as is Earth Seven at noon on a cloudless day.

And as Sslits sat balanced across the peak of the roof, the images of its K'huprician city/mound rose up in its cellular memory and the phantom of three blazing hot suns as Sslits waited for Spashs, the executioner, and death.

And as it sat, and in its cellular mind, four Hive rose up from a camouflaged exit in the top of its city/mound. Each wore a ridged carapace over its back.

And Sslits was one of the four at a corner of a sled that it was pushing along the surface of the planet until all four reached the center of the mound. Spashs was at a corner opposite Sslits. On that sled was the decaying corpse of a member of the things called Sslits, of Hive.

When the sled was in place, a long, thin tube, a proboscis, snaked out from Sslits and from Spashs and from the other two monstrous creatures and attached like suckers to the corpse. Each of the four Sslits began to suck the dead corpse dry. Not because they were cannibalistic or because they shared no kinship whatsoever with the dead, but because each liquid drop was utterly priceless on their desolate world.

Finally satiated, Spashs withdrew its proboscis, looked at Sslits, and said, Celestes.

And suddenly Sslits was back on the roof of Cain's Ballroom and saw everything Spashs saw three blocks away: Jake kneeling by Wood as Wood clutched his crotch on the floor near Celeste who was bound to a chair that lay on its side, and Steve firing a thing in his shaking hand at Spashs. And Sslits heard everything that Spashs heard:

Celestes

Sslits saw blood on Celeste's face.

And Sslits rose up from the apex of the roof, Shirley's face melting into rage. Shirley's hair now a long, red shock of spiked hair like wheat blown in a violent wind that sprang up and back from Sslits forehead and back to the nape of its red neck.

It heard Celeste yell, "Sslits!" just as all K'hupricians heard, in its teeming cellular mind.

Although she did not know it, her microphone and receiver/broadcaster had never been needed to communicate with Sslits.

In that instant, the alien's two massive legs merged into one, the K'huprician dropped its enormously muscled arms to its sides, and the alien exploded up like a powerful waterspout, gushing up; its chest expanding, doubling in size as it rose, gushed up five, ten, then fifteen feet, its back arching as it rose, silhouetted against the moon, until...

It plunged down off of the roof of Cain's ballroom to the street below.

Its metamorphic visage was now the snarling, spitting, fanged face of a raging, Rosicrucian Freddy Kruger.

•••

"This thing is heavy," Lisa Ferry said in her native tongue. She griped as she alternately shrugged her left and then her right shoulder in protest of the straps that held the heavy tank on her back. A hose ran from it to the rod of the flame thrower held under her left arm pit. With her right hand, she quietly closed the back door to the black van without her eyes ever leaving the backside of Spashs steaming across Archer Street towards the Tribune building.

"This really stinks. Why didn't you give this thing to Cowboy or George, for God's sake, and let me carry the machine gun or, better yet, the grenades."

Pariah smiled and answered her in their native language.

"We argue like an old married couple, eh, Lisa. I guess that's because we are an old married couple. Gripe, gripe, gripe, you'd complain if I hung you with a new rope, as the Americans say."

Lisa ignored him. "I don't get it why that, that thing, has to go after her first, either."

Firoz took her free hand and drew it up to his cheek. He rubbed it gently there.

"Because that thing made me whole, Lisa. Clean. If it told me to jump off of a cliff, I'd do it without a question. We wouldn't even be married if I hadn't stumbled on that thing, like you call it, ten or eleven years ago, and if it hadn't erased the cankers and weeping sores all over me. How can you forget that? I was dying, for Kali's sake."

Pariah took her by the hand and led her around the side of the van.

"Now, get the lead out. We need to catch up with Cowboy and George, honey."

As she allowed herself to be led by her husband, she asked, "And tell me again why we have to face that thing's twin, again? We didn't kill it the first time around."

"And we aren't going to kill it this time either. We are supposed to slow it down until Spashs gets here and does the deed."

"That doesn't even make any sense."

Waiting for the arguing couple, Cowboy and George turned towards Firoz and Lisa as they approached.

Pariah sighed. "I guess you weren't listening again. We don't question, we just do. Now, hurry up, please.

"Death waits for no man."

Lisa looked at her husband as if she were enduring the ranting of an idiot.

Pariah shrugged his shoulders and grinned. "I heard that in a movie once."

Ignoring him, Lisa said, "Then, thank God I'm a woman."

CHAPTER THIRTY ONE

"I don't like this, Eric; not one bit," Don Richmond said as added the bulky flashgun to the expensive camera already in his leather bag.

The old man with the furrowed face sat placidly on a cheap chair made out of fake leather in a cheap room in the Route 66 Motel, about ten miles from downtown Tulsa. The motel was located on east Eleventh Street, a segment of the old Route 66 that had once united America, east with west. But tension was thick between the two men; they were far from united themselves.

Eric Gaines ignored Richmond and said, "Help me out of this piece of junk and into my wheelchair, will you. Is everything packed and ready?"

Richmond slung the leather camera case over his shoulder and stepped over to Eric's wheelchair. As he did so, he said, "Everything except the weapon. This is dangerous. Really dangerous. We could both be killed."

He pushed the wheelchair over to Eric's chair where the old man was already rising to make the transfer of his crippled body to the mobile chair.

"Nothing worth doing is without its pitfalls, Richmond. You, of all people, should certainly know that. What we will do today will take the whole world by storm. We will be rich men after today, Don. Rich. Isn't that enough?"

Gaines struggled into the wheel chair as he said, "Now get the weapon, will you. I want to keep it with me the whole time. By my calculations, we're about ten minutes from the Brady district, so let's hurry."

Richmond walked over to the bed where a long canvas bag, tied with string, lay. Inside was the K'huprician weapon.

"I'll go ahead and put that in the car, then come back and get you, Mr. Gaines."

"You'll do nothing of the kind. I'll carry it on my lap. I told you, it is not leaving my sight until our little mission is finished, Don.

"Your photographs will finally prove the existence of an alien on Earth, vindicating me and you and every member of the AAIM. Well worth the personal risk."

Richmond, his discontent clearly etched on his face, handed the weapon to Gaines.

"You look distressed, Don. Remember, you are better than well paid. Not to mention your dedication of our cause. Are you having second thoughts?"

"No, no, no. I'm just trying to think of every angle. You've told me time and again that thing, that alien, can tear a man apart, limb from limb, without raising a sweat."

Don began to push the wheelchair to the apartment's door.

"Yes, yes, that's what this is for, you know. If it tries to attack you while you are taking pictures, or attack me, it knows exactly what this can do to him, so this will protect us while you take the shots.

That was the lie.

•••

In Celeste's room in the Tribune building, Steve said, "Damn!" and swallowed his wad of chewing tobacco.

Dianne cried out, "Sslits!!" although she knew it was hopeless to do so.

In that doorway, Spashs hissed, *CELESTES.*

Wood, rising on one knee and one hand, did not see the horror, but he heard the report of the hand gun as Steve fired. The bullets passed harmlessly through Spashs and out of the open doorway behind it. As Wood painfully rose, he followed those barking retorts to the doorway.

He saw the thing raise its weapon in the hands of its lower set of arms.

In the corner of his eye, he saw Jake raise his hand gun.

His face drained of blood as he heard Spashs say, *It's show time* and saw the alien take along step towards him.

Standing, but still unsteady on his feet, Wood shoved his left hand into the left pocket of his pants. He removed and raised that hand; it held a grenade.

Jake emptied his gun with no effect on the horror.

As Spashs took that first step and Jake fired and Wood threatened, Celeste followed the path of Wood's eyes.

She whispered, "Oh, my God, another…!"

His voice raw with fear, Wood yelled at the red maggot, "This is a grenade!"

Celeste struggled against the ropes that bound her and screamed, "STOP!!!" at everyone and no one.

Wood threw the grenade.

Wood fell to the floor and covered his head with his hands.

Instinctively, Steve threw both of his hands over his face.

It did him no good.

Frozen in fear, Jack did nothing.

Bound, Celeste could only close her eyes and try to turn her face away.

The concussion grenade exploded with terrific force.

The concussion from the explosion picked up the overturned ice chest and the remaining two propane lamps, and the two folding chairs, and threw them violently against the walls.

Like a water-filled balloon dropped from a high window and exploding on impact with the ground, Spashs exploded, its weapon falling, clattering to the floor.

With terrific force, Jake was tossed like a rag doll against the south wall.

Steve was thrown like a dirty tissue against the exterior wall.

Then a dead silence fell over the room broken only by Charles Wood moaning on the floor.

Spashs tottered one step in front of the open doorway; the door hung crazy by one hinge. A jagged half of the alien was gone, splattered on the ceiling and both the north and south walls, and on Celeste's face.

On the floor, Wood looked up at the half unhuman horror, his face glowing with an irrational, triumphant smile.

Like drops of mercury slowly sucked back to their source, the glops of Spashs that had been blown asunder began to gather back and to meld into Spashs as the triumph on Wood's face slowly melted away.

CHAPTER THIRTY TWO

Almost at the corner of Main and Brady, Pariah, Lisa, and their two hired thugs stopped at the muffled sound of the explosion at the Tribune half a block behind them.

"What the hell was that?" asked Lisa, turning to look south, down the street.

Pariah said, "I don't know and it doesn't matter. We've got a job to do and we're going to do it. Cowboy, George, keep it moving."

With an angry sweep of an arm, he waved them forward.

Firoz was several steps north of her before Lisa turned to ignore the mystery behind her, and trotted up to join him. She swore about what Pariah could do to himself under her breath.

At the muffled sound of the explosion, a night watchman at one of the old Main Street warehouses looked up from the copy of the Tulsa World newspaper that he was reading.

The name tag on his shirt read: Stan Lieberman.

He threw his newspaper on the floor, and drew his sidearm.

Cautiously, he walked to the front door of the warehouse and peeked outside. He didn't look far, just enough to be able to tell his boss that he did so tomorrow and still earn a paycheck, then closed and locked the door behind him.

He returned to his desk, picked up the scattered newspaper from the floor, and resumed reading the latest exploits of Charlie Brown and Lucy.

•••

Self-absorption almost complete, the alien horror of pustulant human heads that scarred its body, and claws, and teeth, and multiple flailing arms, that faced Wood and Jake and Celeste, reached down and snatched up the fat, twisted licorice that had been blown free of it by the explosion of the grenade.

Open-mouthed and his face a mask of fear mixed with disbelief and indecision, Wood struggled to rise from the floor.

Gnashing its teeth and nearly completely healed, Spashs aimed its weird, alien weapon. Jake struggled up from the floor next to the wall where he had been thrown by the blast.

Spashs patted the top side of the silver licorice three times.

Still bound to it, Celeste threw herself and her chair to her right side, hard, and down to the floor, bruising her right arm black and blue and knocking her unconscious.

An incredibly intense, soundless, searing beam of light discharged out of the tip of the alien weapon. Aiming at Wood, the alien's discharge went wide and missed its mark.

With not a second to even scream or raise his arms defensively, Jake evaporated in the searing pencil-thin stream of light.

The exterior wall of the room behind Jake exploded out with horrific force, brick and mortar and steel disintegrating into red hot dust and shards.

•••

Almost at the corner of Main and Cameron, one block short of Cain's Ballroom, Lisa stopped in mid-step at the sound of the explosion.

She hissed, "What was that?"

She grabbed her husband by the forearm, stopping him in mid-step.

Cowboy and George stopped as well.

Pariah snarled, "Dammit!! Not again!!" jerked his arm free, and waved her and his two henchmen forward.

•••

As Charles Wood continued to scream, Spashs grabbed him by both sides of his head and lifted him off of the floor.

Spashs slowly squeezed its pseudo-human hands together like a thumb and first digit squeezing a pimple.

Wood's scream grew louder and louder and louder until it was cut short…when his head exploded.

Celeste lay dazed on the floor, free of the now shattered chair, her lips pressed tightly together, her heart barely beating, oblivious to the alien monster that now stood over her as a gelatinous proboscis snaked out from its Kali body and began to stroke her face, her torso, her arms as if it was searching for broken bones or bloody wounds.

The floor, Spashs, and her face were splattered with bloody pieces of Wood.

Separating its fingers of goo, it slowly pushed two up her nostrils even as she twisted her head back and forth in an effort to stop it, and then forced three down her throat as she gagged.

Spashs hissed *Celestes* as she struggled to breathe and her body began to wildly thrash and flop about on the floor for ten, then twenty, then thirty seconds…until she convulsed, and jerked, and lay still.

Spashs removed its fingers leaving long lines of spittle behind. At the touch of its hand on her cheek, Celeste's head rolled limply onto her right shoulder.

Spashs rose and picked up Celeste's limp body, cradling it like a bag of wet flour in the crook of its lower left arm.

The alien horror with the visage of Kali's face and body stood for some moments looking at the chaos that had once been Celeste's room, at furniture overturned or broken, at the dead bodies that had once been human beings, and then lumbered to the still smoking, gaping hole in the wall. The smell of charred wood was everywhere.

A rain of bricks and motor and thick webs of metal littered the sidewalk at the mouth of the hole.

Head thrown back, three of its pseudo-fists clenched while its twisted licorice hung from its fourth, Spashs soundlessly screamed:

Sslits!!!

CHAPTER THIRTY THREE

Headed north and walking just shy of the corner of Cameron and Main, one block from of Cain's Ballroom, Pariah lifted his left arm and hissed, "Stop!"

Despite his intentions, the sound of his voice carried further than he had hoped in the silence of descending twilight on the otherwise deserted street. Even their footfalls on the cement sounded like muffled firecrackers.

He waved Cowboy and George to his side where Lisa waited for instructions. All were painted by heavy shadows as the last vestiges of the sun sank beneath the horizon and the last of daylight evaporated into night.

He said, "Cowboy, you take the sidewalk opposite, George, you take the middle of the street; Lisa will stick with me."

Cowboy said, "Goldurnnit, you can count on me," took off his Stetson and slapped it against his thigh. He liked to pretend he was a cowboy movie star.

Then he and George nodded their assent and left them.

Lisa pulled herself intimately against Pariah's side, bit her knuckle, and begged, "Let's get the hell out of here, baby."

As they slowly trudged up Main Street, Pariah and his team of blackguards did not hear Spashs scream *Sslits!* inside of Sslits cellular mind.

They did not hear their own hearts beating wildly in their heaving chests as, in blind rage, its head down, its eyes up, the raging alien with the Freddy Kruger face, gnashing teeth, and the spiked hair blown back by a nonexistent wind, stomped south down Main Street thirty yards away approaching the intersection with Cameron.

But Pariah saw.

To his fellow rat pack, he yelled, "There it is, and it's ready to blow!"

Sslits did not see the decaying buildings around it, or the pockmarked sidewalk beneath its faux feet, or the darkening twilight above its head. It saw only four threatening meat bags, two weapons, the bazooka and the flame thrower, that were still lodged in its cellular memory, and the image of Celeste bleeding and lying bound to a chair on the floor superimposed over all.

Cowboy was the first of the four to attack.

He felt no fear, only revulsion, at the sight of the monstrous bag of mucous; after all, they had all seen their own alien slug many times before and had become numb to it, and theirs was even more disgusting than the thing facing him.

Cowboy whispered, "...good god..." and began to trot towards Sslits.

Screaming at the top of his lungs, and swinging his machine gun to his left and his right as he ran, the Thompson burped bullets that passed harmlessly through the K'huprician, killing only millions of the billions of its symbiotic squirming cells, to pock-mark bricks and shatter windows in the buildings to the left and behind the alien.

Cowboy sprayed everything before him with deadly lead as thirty yards became twenty and then ten.

At five yards, Sslits flung its massive left arm down and then up and across its torso, forming and hurtling nails of hard water as it did so, nails that, fired like the bullets of a gun, leaving a pattern of bloody holes in Cowboy. He looked down at his torso in surprise as blood began to spurt from the wounds.

Cowboy staggered back and dropped his machine gun.

Then the punctured thug fell with a sickening thud to the ground, dead.

Almost at the same time and only a few feet behind and to the right of Cowboy, George yelled "HEY!" pulled the pin of a grenade and threw it at Sslits even as he leapt to one side of the alien. Hitting the road with his shoulder, he grunted "Unh!" rolled several feet away, and lay curled in a fetal position on the sidewalk, his hands covering his head.

But the memory of knobby grenades moiled black in its cellular mind and, instinctively, Sslits sidestepped the tiny, deadly missile.

The grenade struck the edge of a building to the right and behind the alien who had already launched itself towards George. The sound of the explosion and the concussion washed over the alien, almost knocking it off its feet as a cloud of bricks and shards of glass hung, momentarily, in the air and then rained over Sslits and George, still curled up on the road.

Watching it happen, Lisa stood frozen on the sidewalk barely ten feet away.

Pariah, just behind her and on her right side, fell to his left knee, and, supporting it with his left elbow on his left thigh, aimed his bazooka at the alien.

At the nearby sound of the second explosion that night, Stan Lieberman looked up from his newspaper a second time inside his warehouse.

He cursed, threw the newspaper on the floor, and drew his sidearm again.

He walked briskly to the front door of the warehouse and peeked outside. He didn't have to look far this time, just enough to have everything he believed in to be challenged, then slammed the door closed and locked it behind him.

He returned to his desk and picked up the telephone there, and began to dial the number for the police.

Then he stopped dialing.

He said, "What am I going to tell them?!?"

He replaced the telephone in its cradle and stood up from the desk.

He said, "To Hell with this," and ran out of the warehouse by its back door.

CHAPTER THIRTY FOUR

Kneeling, Pariah yelled, "Lisa!! Lisa!! Pull the trigger!!"

Sslits extended its right clubbed arm with an enlarged fist of hard water, and pulled George's head up from the sidewalk with his left hand.

Surprise and fear owned George's face as the alien embedded the goon's head in the ball of its nauseous mucous.

George began to thrash wildly, fighting to find breath, hands trying and failing to clutch and dislodge the mucous, his horrified face distorted by the gelatinous mass suffocating him.

•••

At that moment, Larry Odom pushed himself partially up from the floor in the Tribune building, shaking splotches of exploding light from his mind, regaining full consciousness.

He looked to his left, but what he saw was hideous and beyond reality and too ridiculous to register on a sane man's mind.

What he saw was the receding back of Kali, the Hindu goddess of death, stepping through a gaping, smoking hole in the exterior wall of Celeste's room. It carried a huge, fat, silver, licorice stick under one of its four arms.

He shook his head again.

Worse yet, he saw the back of Celeste's limp body hanging over the crook of the lower left of four arms of a horror scabbed with a writhing pattern of tiny, human skulls.

He tried to speak, but couldn't, and then the certain hallucination was gone.

Odom staggered to his feet, holding his head between the palms of both of his hands, still confused, and looked around the entire room.

There were bloody pieces of human flesh on the floor, a puzzle that his mind was barely able to reassemble until it did and Odom realized the pieces were the headless body of Charles Wood. Broken and overturned furniture cluttered the room. Jake and Steve's mangled bodies lay like twisted rag dolls against walls.

He couldn't have stopped the torrent of thoughts that almost overwhelmed him as he threw out a hand against the wall next to him to steady himself. *God, in Heaven, what was that thing? Run. Get the hell out. But Celeste...? Call the police. Where's the nearest phone. Get...out! Get the cops; you can't do anything! Where's Celeste...?*

But he purposely slowed his breathing, straightened to his full height, and walked cautiously to the hole torn in the wall by God knew what. The Kali thing?

He looked outside.

Odom withdrew his head, and looked around the room again for something, anything, that he could carry with him for protection, but found nothing.

He looked outside again, and, this time, his love for Celeste Gaines conquered his completely well founded and almost debilitating fear of the known and unknown.

And Larry stepped through the hole.

•••

Fire burning in its unholy eyes, the K'huprician monster that had just murdered the lifeless muddle of flesh under it on the sidewalk looked up and at Lisa.

Lisa gasped; tears welling up in her eyes as she faced not only a nameless monstrosity from the stars but her own certain death.

She managed to whisper, "Firoz…" once as she pulled the trigger on the flame thrower, then pulled it again, and again, and again.

Nothing happened.

Parish yelled, "LISA!!!" and fired the bazooka.

Because his hands shook violently, the shot went wide and its rocket shot over Sslits, arched over the street behind the alien, and exploded on the sidewalk in front of Cain's Ballroom.

Sslits took two sloshing steps towards Lisa who yelped as it reached out and yanked the flame thrower from her hands. In doing so, the heavy tank on her back was almost jerked off, pulling her entire body off center, to her right and almost off of her feet.

Pariah whispered, "Lisa", and dropped his bazooka.

Sslits picked up Lisa by both of her shoulders, held her in front of his snarling, mangled Kruger face for a heartbeat as she slobbered and wept and struggled in his grip, and then jerked her head into its chest.

Pariah, yelped, turned, and ran as Lisa's body squirmed and twisted and hung from the middle of the K'huprician's torso.

The alien grabbed her struggling body by the waist and crammed her deeper, then deeper, again into its torso.

His face streaming with tears, and his chest heaving from exertion, Pariah ran south down Main Street, never looking back.

Lisa's body stopped squirming. Sslits pulled Lisa's dead body out.

Pariah looked up and south down Main Street as he ran, his face red from the exertion, his eyes and cheeks red with tears as he ran to save himself.

Sslits looked at Lisa's dead body with no discernible emotion and then dropped it to the sidewalk like a child bored with a toy.

Pariah tried to stop before colliding with what he saw step out onto

Main Street from Brady just yards in front of him. He tried to stop so flat footed that he staggered forward in mid-flight, tripping on his own feet, crying out, throwing his hands up and out for balance, until he did stumble to a clumsy stop.

The thing that stopped him, that held a weapon in one set of arms and Celeste in the second of four arms, that stood at the edge of Main Street and leered from its face of death at its own East Indian bottom feeder, said, *Pariahs.*

•••

At the moment that Pariah and his henchmen had confronted Sslits, just shy of the intersection of Cameron and Main, Don Richmond slowed his sedan to a crawl and pulled over to the sidewalk on the north side of Cameron just east of Main. His hands were trembling on the steering wheel.

His camera case sat on its bench seat between him and Eric Gaines. Gaines' wheelchair was folded up in the backseat next to the alien weapon wrapped in canvas. Gaines looked as if he were distracted by memories or lost in thought.

Richmond turned the key to the ignition off and said, "This is insanity."

Calmly and without looking at Don, Eric responded, "We don't have time to go over this again, Don. There is absolutely nothing to worry about. My contact says that Sslits is very near. We won't have far to go. So, please, get my wheelchair out."

At that moment, they heard the muffled explosion of the grenade thrown at Sslits about half-a-block away.

"What was that?" asked Don, clutching the steering wheel of the sedan.

"I don't know, Don, but my guess is that Sslits is very near indeed. Hurry."

"No, I've changed my mind. I won't do it."

Eric turned to face him, his face, a contradiction of emotions, both serious, calm and excited, his eyes somehow bright.

He sighed deeply. "Then I'm afraid that I'll have to play my last card, Don. I don't have any more time to waste. I'm sorry; I never wanted to do this. But I have a file on an activity that you were involved in several years ago that, I'm afraid, you really don't want turned over to the police, my boy."

As the blood drained from his face, Don asked, "What are you talkin' about?"

" THE THING... SAID PARIAHS."

"It has to do with your curious and aberrant fondness for little boys…"

"Shut up!!" Don yelled. "Shut up!! How did you…?"

"It doesn't really matter how, does it, only that I have it. Now, get the wheelchair, Don."

Scared almost out of his wits and with a growing fury, Don exited the driver's side of the sedan and walked around it to the door to its back seats. He opened that door, took out the wheelchair, and unfolded it. Then he leaned across the backseat and dragged the long canvas bag out by one end. He propped it up against the side of the sedan.

Eric had already opened his door and was waiting impatiently; he had already swung his legs outside of the sedan with some effort. He said, "Hurry, hurry, Don. It's not like I can wheel that thing at fifty miles an hour."

Don unfolded and then placed the wheelchair in front of Eric, and, helping to pull him into the chair by Gaines's armpits, situated the head of AAIM into a comfortable position.

Impatient and excited, Eric commanded, "The weapon, Don, the weapon. Give it."

Don placed the canvas wrapped weapon across Eric's lap, walked to the back of the wheelchair, and began to push it. Its wheels, badly in need of oil, objected to his effort.

"I'm not sure," Eric enthused, "that you really understand the full import of what is happening right now, Don, and I do understand your fear."

He patted the canvas bag twice, and only twice.

"But you have nothing to fear…"

CHAPTER THIRTY FIVE

They heard but did not see the rocket that went wide and overshot Sslits, heard it as it arched over the street behind the alien, and exploded.

Eric grabbed a wheel in each hand and began to vigorously push himself along at a greater speed, almost pulling the wheelchair out of Don's hands, his mind so focused that he saw nothing around him as he was overcome by the flow of adrenaline in his body.

"This is it!" he gashed as he pushed. "This is it!

"I've waited so long!! Eric…!"

He glanced over his shoulder.

He stopped pushing the wheels of his chair, swirling it partially around instead to watch Don's backside as his panicked aide ran down the sidewalk back towards the sedan.

Eric started to shout, but the word died on his lips. He knew it was useless.

He swiveled his squeaking wheelchair back to face the intersection of Main Street and Cameron, just a yard or two in front of him, as he muttered to himself.

Under his breath, he said, "Coward."

•••

Leering with a bear's trap of exposed, exaggerated teeth, and using a free hand, Spashs slowly raised Celeste's limp body from the crook of its lower, left arm.

It used the chuckle, almost like a cackle in its faux throat that it had learned from the laugh tracks of American sitcoms shown in India as it raised her bloody body level with its torso.

Then the K'huprician executioner dropped Celeste with a sickening and final thud to the street in front of it and began taking long, slimy steps towards Sslits.

Inside and outside of Spashs cellular mind, Sslits screamed, *No!!!* and stepped towards Celeste's twisted body, crumpled on the street behind Spashs like a puppet with cut strings.

Spashs gurgled *Yes* with an evil sneer, then hissed again *Yes*.

Spashs raised its twisted licorice weapon.

It was then that Sslits lunged, striking the weapon out of the alien's hand, sending it clattering to the street where it spun and spun and spun until it struck Celeste's body where she lay just north of the intersection of Main and Brady.

It was then that Sslits threw a punch with its right fist that sunk up to its wrist in Spashs' Kali face, that knocked the K'huprician back, that instantly renewed their shared Hive minds in an explosion of dark, crackling, energy globes bursting like multi-colored bubbles in Sslits cellular mind.

And Sslits saw in that seconds long vision the timeless city/mound that was Hive, and, inside it, the gathered ruling council of pustulant bags of mucous called Sslits, and heard the chaos of psychic images thrown about among the minds of these Sslits arguing about what to do with the Hive traitor on Earth Seven until it was decided to execute that traitor, and the council fell silent in compromise, and there was Spashs among them, leering, and then a lone, silver disk silently rose from the city/mound that had been Sslits entire reality to disappear up, up, up into the pale green sky ablaze with three suns.

Then Sslits pulled its fist free of Spashs face, trailing goo in its wake.

Now hissed Spashs as it staggered back, in the process of reforming its mangled face, *we are Hive again. And Spashs harvests Sslits.* And *Spashs knows all Sslits knows.*

But Sslits burbled NO!

•••

When Larry Odom reached the northeast corner of Archer and Main as the sun completely disappeared beneath the horizon, he did not hear the first words spoken by the second alien that he'd ever seen, nor the words spoken aloud by Sslits.

What he saw however, stopped him dead in his tracks. It was the backside of a four-armed alien horror covered with sores like human skulls that, facing Sslits crouching like a wrestler, dropped Celeste's body on the street.

Odom winched at the sound.

As Sslits slapped the alien weapon from the monster it faced, and that weapon spun away until it struck Celeste's body lying in the street, Odom knew that the decision he would have to make in the next few seconds would change the rest of his life.

Forever.

Lowering its Kali head and folding its four arms around its torso, Spashs lunged at Sslits.

It struck the K'huprician in its midsection and hurling the alien and it both back, stumbling back, trying desperately but failing to find purchase on the sidewalk, barely missing a fire hydrant, struggling to free themselves from one another until both slammed into and through the oversized, double, wooden doors in the building behind them. Those doors splintered as the K'huprician's massive bodies fell with in a wet thrashing tangle on the dusty, concrete floor of the long abandoned warehouse.

CHAPTER THIRTY SIX

The second that Odom saw the bodies of the aliens fall into and through the gaping hole in the warehouse doors, he broke into a measured lope meant to eat up distance without exhausting him. Now unafraid of being seen, gritting his teeth and clenching the muscles of his jaws as he pushed his fear down, Odom determined to reach Celeste's body where it lay like a twisted, bloody doll in the street without being seen.

As he ran, and one by one, he caught glimpses of Lisa's corpse and the flame thrower's tank on the east side of Main just south of Cameron, then of the two men lying on the street nearby her that Odom did not recognize but that were certainly both dead.

That told him that his decision to run to Celeste would be the decision that most likely was going to get him killed.

He bit his lower lip and ran anyway.

•••

Leering with its horrific Kali mouth a tangle of teeth, Spashs struggled to its pseudo feet in the murky darkness of the warehouse and hissed: *Sslits betrayed Hive… Sslits must die.*

At that moment, in a telephone booth in front of a disreputable convenience store five miles east of the Brady District, Don Richmond dropped two coins into the telephone's slot and dialed the police. Two slutty young women standing next to the convenience store's entrance gave him the once over look and decided he wasn't worth the money.

Slurring his words somewhat, Don began to report that two monsters were tearing at one another in the Brady District to the female voice on the other end of the line. But thinking better of it, he lied and said there was a gang war starting up right now.

"You people better bring the big guns out," he said, "and someone is going to get killed. He dropped the phone to hang by its cord, he ran back to his car, pulled out of the parking lot of the convenience store, almost backing into a parked car there, and drove away.

He was never seen again.

•••

Sslits pushed itself up by its left forearm as it lay in the dark of the warehouse on the concrete floor and, looking to its right, saw a dusty pile of discarded tools: a length of rusted, coiled chain, a crowbar, a monkey wrench, a discarded, flat tire, and a broken hammer. It stretched out an extended right arm and drew back its fist balled around the crowbar. It threw back its right arm and slung the crowbar with great force.

Spashs saw and tried to jerk itself out of its trajectory as the deadly iron missile hurled at it, but the tool struck and sliced off its uppermost right arm, struck the wall behind the K'huprician and embedded there.

Its severed arm fell to the floor where it squirmed and thrashed as the millions of cellular red maggots inside fought for life, severed from community.

Sslits pushed itself to its feet as Spashs staggered back, desperately trying to stop the flow of precious cellular liquid seeping from the wound in its right shoulder. It sank to its faux knees and retrieved its severed limb. It stuck it over the weeping wound and began to reabsorb it into its body.

As Spashs did so, and balancing its massive weight on its right leg, Sslits kicked out with its left leg.

The heel of its foot struck and cracked Spashs left faux knee.

Spashs screamed in a high whine, in a sound alien to human ears. Its back struck the doorjamb behind it, its body spun to its right, and the K'huprician fell to the ground, laying half in the doorway of the warehouse and half outside on the concrete sidewalk.

Sslits stepped to the interior wall opposite Spashs and wrenched the crowbar out of the wall where it was embedded.

Spashs rolled over and over and over and away from the doorway and into the street, leaving a slimy trail like a snail from its wound in the dust on the floor.

Sslits followed its executioner until, reaching the fire hydrant on the sidewalk at the edge of the street; the alien raised and elongated its right arm above its head, and brought the crowbar down on the top of the fire hydrant with terrific force.

To Sslits' left side, Spashs struggled up to its knees, its left side already self-healed, then rose up to its feet. It balled its three remaining hard-water fists, and thrusting them like a battering ram in front of itself, ran at Sslits.

With pile-driver force, it struck Sslits in its torso, throwing the stumbling alien backwards and knocking the crowbar out of its hand.

Spashs followed Sslits as it staggered backwards, fighting to maintain balance, and the K'huprician snatched up the crowbar from the street. Spashs struck the top of the hydrant again with even greater force.

•••

At that moment, Odom reached Celeste's body. He picked up the licorice weapon and hurled it with all of his strength at the narrow breezeway between two buildings behind him and Celeste where it struck the northern wall of one of the buildings and disappeared into the aperture.

Quickly kneeling but never moving his eyes off of the two battling aliens, he placed the first two digits of his right hand against her neck in search of a pulse.

Under his breath, he whispered, "C'mon, c'mon, c'mon…"

Looking down at Celeste's fish-belly white face, he pressed his fingers more firmly against her neck.

He whispered, "Celeste, please..." and then stopped whispering.

Odom said, "She's alive…" He removed his fingers from her neck.

He looked up not at the aliens tearing at each other, or at the dead bodies of Lisa, Cowboy, and Fred scattered around Main Street, or even up to God.

He began to cry.

CHAPTER THIRTY SEVEN

As Sslits came at the alien, Spashs struck the top of the hydrant again with incredible force, breaking off the top of the metal plug.

The red metal cap of the broken hydrant was hurled up on the white crest of a thick column of water spewing into the air only to fall with the heavy sound of metal on concrete just feet from Spashs.

Throwing its pseudo-hands up before its pupil-less eyes, Sslits recoiled back onto the sidewalk to escape the horror of the vertical flood of water, recoiling as if it were a deluge of blood, recoiling as if it were drowning in more water than it had ever seen in its thousand years of life.

The geyser roared up, and up, and up, widening and spreading at its apex until it fell apart and became rain that fell to wet the sidewalk and street in a wide circumference around and under it, falling on Odom's tearful upturned face. That rain began to pool in multiple places on Main Street, forming rivulets that began to run down its slight incline.

Ignoring its fear and revulsion, Spashs plunged its torso and head into the terrific upward thrust of the geyser.

That incredible upward thrust fought to throw the alien out of the torrent, but failed.

Spashs unhinged its malleable jaws and opened its exaggerated mouth over the drenching flood. Gulping in great draughts, it began absorbing part of the geyser, inflating, ballooning, bloating as it did so.

As it watched Spashs double its girth, Sslits burbled: Spashs wrong... wrong... wrong.

At that time, heading south down Main Street at forty-five miles an hour, the vintage Indian motorcycle roared out from underneath the overpass just several yards north of Cain's Ballroom. The aging, Asian hippy on that cycle wore a walrus mustache, tied his graying hair back into a pony-tail, and completed his 'look' with the dirty tennis shoes, frayed, cut-off jeans, T-shirt, and do-rag with white stars and red and blue strips that had become a motorcycle cliché. His name was Herbie.

Although he ignored the warning about tobacco along with any other law he didn't like, he equally hated police, all authority, and the federal government in particular with a paranoid passion, the lit cigar clamped in the right corner of his mouth was about to prove that smoking is hazardous to one's health.

As he looked up over the handlebars at the road ahead, his single thought, where to score a joint, instantly evaporated into an open-mouthed, wide-eyed fear at what he saw ahead.

He yelled "Holy sh...!" but the wind caught and carried away the rest of his profanity.

As the hydrant gushed with unabated fury, the grossly bloated Spashs took several steps back from the geyser and hissed: *Ahh.*

It was then that the Indian motorcycle hit one of the gathering pools of water on the street and skidded. The vintage Indian careened, listing heavily to the left as the cyclist frantically fought for control of his bike.

Herbie lost.

He leapt off just as his beloved motorcycle fell over to the pavement on its side, continuing to screech, metal on concrete, as it slid away from him and down the street. The bike's tires left a black skid mark in their wake on the street. The Asian continued to roll over and over and over, losing his do-rag and his still lit cigar as he rolled, until his bruised, limp, and unconscious body abruptly and painfully hit the east side curb on Main.

As the hippy hit the curb, Spashs raised its gigantic upper left arm over its head and transformed it into a great, bloated club and burbled, *die.*

The cycle rammed into Sslits's legs from behind, buckling the K'huprician forward into a partial squat, but doing no real harm. After the brunt of the impact, Sslits turned behind itself to its right and grabbed the heavily damaged cycle with its right hand, and swung it up in front of itself.

In that second, Spashs swung its own huge clubbed arm down like the hammer of Thor, but missed, striking the road left of Sslits with a jarring but useless impact.

Although alien to its own limited knowledge, Sslits grabbed the cycle without hesitation with its left hand as well and swung it up, effortlessly, over its own head and level with the engorged Spashs' Kali face.

Sslits hissed like the sound of air escaping from a balloon and, drawing it back even further, hurled the motorcycle at Spashs.

•••

No one—not Eric Gaines, not Larry Odom, not the night watchman who had already fled the scene, not either of the aliens—heard the distant ululating wail of approaching police sirens.

•••

The twisted motorcycle, hurled like a javelin, sliced through the edge of Spashs's left side, revealing Larry Odom only five yards behind the alien cowering over Celeste with both arms thrown over his face.

Larry Odom dropped his arms and screamed, "*SSLITS!!*"

Herbie, the hippy, lifted himself up on his skinned forearms from where he lay in the gutter, his eyes wide with fear at what he saw but thought was an hallucination, and said, "Holy shit!" as his still lit cigar burned on the sidewalk at the edge of the building behind him.

The Indian cycle sliced through Spashs, knocking the alien back and to one side, and hurtled in a high arch over Larry Odom and Celeste until it smashed into the large, barred, plate-glass window of an old, abandoned restaurant behind them. A large, rusted, metal sign above the front window of the restaurant that had been closed for more than twenty years identified it as *The Lyin' Snake Cafe.*

Odom threw himself over Celeste as the cycle flew by overhead, and choked at the sound of the impact behind him.

As it struck, one of the broken and twisted bars on the window pierced the gas tank of the Indian, sending a stream of gasoline spewing out from the motorcycle barely hanging there, the gas falling to and then flowing in a narrow stream across the sidewalk towards the street, pooling, and then forming a rivulet of fuel creeping towards the street.

As it did so, Herbie felt for his cigar in the corner of his mouth out of long habit until, not finding it there, he looked behind him for his stogie.

He looked just as the foremost edge of the thin stream of gas reached the glowing tip of his cigar. His face drained of blood. The trademark profanity on his lips was never spoken.

The fuel ignited and ran back up the rivulet of fuel falling from the tank of the motorcycle.

The motorcycle exploded in a fireball that shot out and instantly incinerated the Asian in the gutter and funneled over Odom and Celeste.

CHAPTER THIRTY EIGHT

Eric Gaines had been watching the aliens tear at one another from his wheelchair on the corner of Main and Cameron for several minutes when the sound of the explosion reached him and the fireball blossomed out of the front of the building. Instinctively, his face underlit by the explosion and his eyes wide with fear, he began to franticly wheel himself back from the corner.

•••

As the hydrant gushed, Sslits turned towards the raging fire crawling up the side of the building as a great cloud of debris and smoke belched out from the new gaping mouth in *The Lyin' Snake*, momentarily obscuring the burning motorcycle and most everything else, including Spashs, to the alien.

That was when three police cars roared into the intersection of Cameron and Main and three more into the intersection of Brady and Main, their sirens screaming. Six sets of tires screeched as they all spun to a stop, blocking Main from egress or ingress, and twenty-four doors were flung open as if it had all been choreographed.

Twenty-four sets of boots hit the pavement; all of the policemen were armed with rifles, shotguns, or handguns. One of the officers on each end of Main carried a large Walkie-talkie. Captain Theodore "Popeye" Phillips carried the Walkie-talkie on the north end of Main.

One of the policemen behind him said, "I thought someone called in a gang war. What the hell is this?"

Phillips answered, "I don't really know, but whatever it is, our job is to end it, and that's exactly what we're gonna do."

He barked into his Walkie-talkie at his contact on the south end of Main, "Stand down and get out of the line of fire! You're back-up!"

The Police Captain then pulled his model 1026 Smith and Wesson 10mm pistol out of its holster on his hip.

Phillips quickly scanned the scene before him, noting the bodies already dead in the street, and pointed his left arm to the west side of Main. He barked, "Sounds like all Hell's breakin' loose. Get some men on the other side of the street, there! Proceed with extreme caution. I want everyone going home tonight!"

The policeman nearest him carrying a Remington Model 870 Wingmasters shotgun said, "Like these popguns will stop those things."

Another said, "What are those things!?!"

"Movie props," the Captain lied. "How the Hell should I know? Jimmy, get your Parkerized M-14 up on the roof of one of those buildings and aim for something that looks like a head if and when I signal you."

•••

At that moment, Eric Gaines stopped his wheelchair, spun it partially around facing Main Street again, and looked down at the canvas wrapped weapon in his lap. And the hurtful memories, the betrayed love, the destruction of his family, the ridicule and shame he had endured as a 'UFO nut', and the vitriolic legal haggling for miserable decades were dredged up at the sight of Celeste lying bloody in the street. And all of the terror that shook his hands, and the animal instinct to live at all costs, were eaten up by his all-consuming, illogical, painful hatred for the alien bag of pus called Sslits that was slightly weaving back and forth where it stood half a block from him. With his eyes burning with the raw loathing and hatred that was actually for himself but that he projected onto Sslits, Eric began to wheel himself down the west edge of Main Street.

•••

Spashs stepped through the already dissipating smoke of the fire, its three arms transformed into three great serrated claws, its body engorged with water, with life, with power, towering over Sslits.

The time for words was over.

Captain Phillips barked into his Walkie-talkie and he and his remaining men began to advance towards the raging aliens.

When he and his men were a mere eight yards from Sslits and Spashs, Phillips threw up his right hand and the gun there and yelled, "Stop!"

He and his men stopped. The looks on their faces ran the gamut of fear, confusion, consternation, and disbelief at what they saw.

Captain Phillips drew his service revolver and, anchoring it with his left hand under his right fist, pointed it at Sslits and illogically yelled, "FREEZE!!" at the two aliens.

There was no response from either of the animated bags of mucous in the roadway.

Even as he yelled it, Phillips felt stupid. To cover that stupidity, he added, "We need an ambulance....now! Ron, go!!! And get the firemen out here too!

"Robert, check those bodies!"

Robert, gun drawn, spun off from the group.

Ron ran back to one of the patrol cars, plopped down in its bench seat, and snatched the microphone to the vehicle's short-wave radio off of its dash.

As Ron did so, the captain caught sight of Larry Odom standing over a woman's body in the street, waving his arms and yelling, "This woman is still alive...!"

At that second and using two of its serrated claws, Spashs seized Sslits by the throat and began to shake the condemned like a doll as Sslits pressed one of its hands, fingers ridged and extended, against Spashs torso and shot a liquid spike through its executioner's chest.

Surprise distorting its Kali face, Spashs released Sslits' throat, and, staggering backward, tried to seal the weeping liquid at its chest wound with the lowest of its two left claws.

•••

His wheelchair sitting in the middle of the intersection of Main and Cameron, Eric Gaines unwrapped the canvas from the licorice weapon and let the cloth fall to the pavement.

Kneeling by Lisa's body, Ron cupped a hand over his mouth and yelled back at Captain Phillips, "This one's dead!!" Then he rose to trot to the next corpse.

In the growing chaos of movement and sound, Captain Phillips raised his right arm with his gun over his head and signaled his sharpshooter to fire by waving his hand in the form of a broad number 8.

Robert's rifle spat and the bullet struck the back of Spashs head, jerking it forward, then tearing through its left cheek to bury itself in the street.

Although the tiny wound self-healed almost instantly, it and Sslits' water spike seemed to disorient the alien executioner, confusing its focus.

Now driven to blind fury, Spashs lunged again at Sslits, and, grabbing its foe with its massive claws by an arm and leg, lifted Sslits off of the street.

As it raised Sslits, struggling in its grip above its head, it hissed, *Why does Sslits fight?*

There was no answer as engorged Spashs, still almost a third larger than Sslits, and using all of its mustered strength like a hydraulic gun threw Sslits at the wall of the burning building.

Still lying over Celeste, Odom glanced up and back to see Sslits hit the wall next to the tottering, burning motorcycle with bone-jarring force. Jarred lose by the impact, the mangled motorcycle fell to the sidewalk as did Sslits, pulling a great section of the wall around it in a rain of debris that buried the alien in a mound of smoldering brick on the sidewalk as *The Lyin' Snake Café* sign wrenched free of its rusted moorings to the wall and collapsed with the brick.

Spashs threw back its head in triumph and yelled in its alien tongue.

In that moment, Captain Phillips also yelled. He shouted, "Take that big mother down any way you can!" waving his remaining men forward as he ran with a broad sweep of his left arm.

Fighting their way through their own fear and disbelief and firing their weapons in a cacophony of sound, Phillips and his men advanced.

The shots struck and passed through Spashs, drawing the alien's attention away from Sslits, buried under the mound of debris, to the policemen.

Spashs extended an arm like a water cannon and shot a tremendous blast of water that picked up two of Phillips' policemen off of their feet and threw them heavily backwards like wet, crumpled tissue paper to the street while drenching Captain Phillips.

As Phillips tried to shake the blinding water from his stinging eyes, Spashs snatched him up off of the street.

Phillips screamed and dropped his Smith and Wesson and Walkie-talkie.

The south contingent of cops broke into a run towards their Captain and the alien, drawing their weapons.

Spashs raised Phillips, struggling and screaming in its grip, in both of its claws and broke him in two.

Phillips' scream was cut off as bricks on the mound of debris behind Odom and Celeste were pushed up from beneath to tumble down with a clatter onto the sidewalk.

The remaining policemen running north on Main began to fire their Smith and Wesson revolvers, rifles, and shotguns as they ran.

A liquid glop beneath the bricks rose into a small hump on the mound and bubbled up through any crack there, taking on a vaguely humanoid shape as it separated itself from the steaming debris.

Until the rising hump on the bricks was Sslits.

Spashs turned to face the police as they fired and ran.

Pulling ahead of his fellows, the policeman closest to Spashs did not live to regret it.

As he cursed and spat and fired his hand gun point blank into Spashs gut, the alien effortlessly popped off his head.

The remaining police stopped dead in their tracks and recoiled in horror, still firing.

Sslits turned to the *The Lyin' Snake Cafe* sign half pulled off of the wall behind the alien from its metal anchoring. It seized it by the lower hanging letters Y and F and tore it off of the wall.

Larry startled and ran, and as he ran north, saw Eric Gaines with the alien licorice weapon in his wheel chair about thirty feet in front of him.

He saw Eric raise the weapon.

Sslits, enraged in mindless fury, lifted the huge, rusting, metal sign, still trailing some electrical wires, over its head as the alien ran at Spashs.

Larry said, "Oh, God," as he doubled his speed. He didn't need any additional clue to tell him who was the target of that weapon.

Out loud, he yelled, "Eric!! NO!!!"

Eric turned to Larry's voice, and a cracked smile spread across his mouth.

"Well, well, well, what a pleasant surprise."

He did not lower the weapon.

Instead, he gently tapped the top of the weapon once.

Sslits threw the massive *Lyin' Snake* sign.

As he ran, Larry screamed, "Eric, NO!!!"

Eric gently tapped the top of the weapon again.

The sign struck Spashs squarely in the middle of its torso, throwing the alien executioner back on its heels.

Larry lunged at Eric.

Eric gently tapped the top of the weapon a third time.

Larry tackled Eric, knocking the wheelchair over, carrying them both over to strike the pavement with a jarring *thud*.

As they toppled over a pencil thin, searing ray of yellow light instantly shot out of its tip.

It struck Spashs as the sign struck Spashs, and Spashs screamed and exploded...splattering on the police still firing their weapons, splattering on the pavement around it in a ragged circle of goo, and splattering on Sslits slowing to a stop not three feet from what had been Spashs.

Sslits said, Spashs.

Then Sslits jerked its head slightly to the side and behind it as if it heard something.

Sslits said, Celestes!

Odom rolled free of Eric and the overturned wheelchair, and jumped to his feet. In a heartbeat, he snatched the weapon from Eric and threw it with all of his strength behind them.

Then he kicked Eric in the head where he lay, partially beneath his wheelchair, unmoving and unconscious.

As Sslits began to lumber toward Celeste, what had just happened awakened the police from a psychological paralysis, and they raised their weapons again.

Yelling and waving his arms like a mad man, Odom also began to run towards Celeste, screaming, "Don't shoot!! Don't shoot! He won't hurt her!!!"

The police began to lower their weapons as much out of not knowing what to do as for any other reason as they caught sight of Odom. Indeed, they took several steps back as both the lawyer and the monster reached the body of the woman on the street.

Sslits never even looked at Larry Odom as carefully, slowly, reverently, it knelt and then lay down, slowly engulfing Celeste's body as it sank over her.

Like fruit in Jell-O Odom thought.

Sslits closed its pseudo-eyes as it immersed Celeste.

Glistening with life. Reborn. Rejuvenated. New.

When it had completely swallowed up Celeste in itself, Odom watched with expectation to see the fish belly white flesh of her face melt away to be replaced by the pink of life, to see her instinctively gasp for air, her lungs filling instead and once more with ever greater dollops of Sslits' goop until her lungs were saturated and she were healed, restored to complete health.

Moments crawled by like centuries as Odom watched Celeste's body relax. Relax. Relax.

Then Sslits belched.

Then the alien began to roll off of Celeste, trailing long lines of alien spittle from itself to her body until it lay completely by her side on the road, the alien monster arduously beginning to regenerate its damaged pseudo-human face and arms and legs and feet until its metamorphosis was complete.

And Odom knelt by Celeste, his face alive with anticipation.

He placed the first two fingers of his right hand on her neck.

CHAPTER THIRTY NINE
TUESDAY, DEC. 17TH, 4:30PM 1996
TULSA OKLAHOMA SAFE 'HOUSE'

The half-empty bottle of Double Cola was sweating in Eric's hand as he wheeled his chair down the hallway of the *Route 66 Western Motel* on the edge of Tulsa. He was convinced that, despite how great the first half had tasted, the second half would taste even better.

But the cold soda pop was really of little consolation for the misery

" DON'T SHOOT!   HE WON'T HURT HER! "

he had endured for days holed up in the smarmiest motel in which he had ever stayed in his entire life. The police had placed him in this 'safe house' until he could be safely arraigned for Spashs's murder. It was 'for his own protection' from the crackpots and worse who had been caught up in the worldwide furor over the greatest breaking news in the history of the world. He was prepared for a long stay. He only wished that the police had had a better budget.

The faded brown baseboards were peeling away from the motel wall in random places, the pattern in the colorless carpet had been worn down to obscurity and there were occasional small rips in it, and the lighting thrown from the few bare light bulbs hanging from the ceiling cast yellow light and wavering shadows over the entire mess.

At least he had seen no spiders.

The only thing more shoddy in the hall was the fat, plainclothes policeman sitting in a chair tipped back on its hind legs against the wall next to Eric's room. His name was Jimmie Pummell, and he was too busy reading a copy of the tabloid newspaper, *The Global Star,* to even pretend to care that Eric was approaching. He looked like an unmade bed; his cap was pushed back over a high forehead revealing the beginnings of male pattern baldness. His chin was grey from stubble.

The headline on the tabloid newspaper's front page read:

ALIEN LOVE CHILD
DIES IN BIRTH
By Ace Montana

At least, the photograph beneath the headline was authentic and was of Sslits. Eric guessed he'd finally seen the last of the little green men from Mars myth.

In a flat voice, he said, "Hello, Pummell," as he passed the policeman guarding his room with no intention of saying anything else, but the headline was too great a temptation. So he stopped in front of the cop with not much anticipation of anything approaching an enlightening or satisfying conversation.

He said, "You shouldn't believe everything you read, Jimmie. You can read, can't you?"

Jimmie looked up from the tabloid.

"Oh, hello, Mr. Gaines. I was just reading about that alien thing that's in all the papers and on all of the TV shows. Damn. I never thought I'd see the day. Why does its face look like Paul McCartney?"

An invisible light bulb went on over Jimmie's head.

"But, say, you'd be the expert on that stuff, now wouldn't you? That's why you're here in the first place, for killing one of them things!"

Ignoring the last statement, Eric said, "You know, Jimmie, you are one sorry guard. If I were still in the CIA, I'd have your butt fired with the snap of a finger."

"What are you talking about? Someone shoot you, Mr. Gaines?"

"No."

"Someone stick a knife in you at the vending machine?"

"Obviously not."

"Then I'd say I'm doing my job with one hundred and ten percent efficiency."

Eric sighed.

"Could you at least take a moment from expanding your mind to unlock my door, Jimmie? I'm tired, I've got a nice bottle of rum waiting for me, and I sure would appreciate it."

"I never locked it."

Eric studied the vapid grin on Jimmie's face and judged that he had about one chance in Hell of surviving his sequestration.

He opened the door with his free hand, then wheeled his chair into the room.

"Stupid, stupid me," he added, then closed the door after him and locked it. He jiggled the doorknob to make sure it was locked.

The shabby room was just as he had left it. The bed was unmade; he saw no need to make it since the whole purpose of a safe house was to make sure he had no visitors, unexpected or otherwise. A cloth-bound chair sat next to the left side of the bed, and next to that, a small table. On that table was an unopened and half-empty bottle of rum, an empty glass, and a folded copy of the current issue of the *Tulsa Tribune* newspaper. There was a low and small chest-of-drawers that held what few possessions he had been allowed, a door leading to what passed for either a closet or a bathroom, and nothing more. There was no window. The walls were companion to two faded, framed prints of something colorful, faded, and abstract.

Eric rolled to the chair, placed the drink on the end table, and then, with a great deal of effort, got himself out of his wheelchair and down in the cloth chair. He poured Double Cola into the glass, and then rum. He took a long, slow sip, and then sat the glass back among the ring stains on the table.

He knew he shouldn't be ungrateful. If not for the worst legal entanglement in the history of jurisprudence brought about by the destruction of 'persons' and property in the Brady District, including the ongoing debate over the pending legal status of whether he had killed an unthinking animal or a foreign representative of another 'country' with immunity from the law (thanks to the legal brilliance of Larry Odom), he would have already been in jail. But he was ungrateful and much more.

It felt like every muscle in his body was bruised, although that wasn't possible, and every bone was weary. He was, after all, an old man now. So, with one eye on hitting the sack early, Eric picked up the newspaper. The headline in the largest type he'd ever seen on a newspaper read: ALIENS ARE REAL.

He imagined that that or variations of that headline had been repeated in every newspaper, on every radio station, and on every television on earth in the last weeks.

He opened it to page four and a sidebar story there with a byline he didn't recognize. But, then, he didn't need to recognize it. He knew that Odom had sold Celeste's diary in bits and dribbles to a syndicate that had sold it worldwide.

The diary under the headline and sidebar read:

From the Journal of Celeste Gaines, Sept. 9, 1947.

Since the creature's removal from its space ship at the Roswell, New Mexico crash site, the singular most amazing event in human history has been a comedy of errors. It killed Johnathan Staloone today. He was attempting to obtain a sample of the goop making up this creature, using a hypodermic needle. He had taken every precaution in the book. He wasn't a stupid man at all. He was a college educated, highly trained and dependable technician.

Yet, it slaughtered Staloone like a man would bat a fly. Without warning. Without emotion. Without any perceivable motive. The video cameras in the lab caught it all on film.

Then it drank him. There's nothing left. No flesh. No shard of bone. If the cameras hadn't caught it, we would have thought he had just gone

Maybe it thought Staloone was a threat. I don't know. How could I know?

Maybe it was right. Maybe Stallone did something to hurt it, or irritate it, or scare it.

The official story released to the few who would even want to know what happened to him is that Staloone was burned in a military helicopter crash. His family will be taken care of; cheaper than lawsuits.

So the lies continue. Making matters worse—the alien is beyond containment, actually. How do you jail water? Thank God it obviously doesn't know that.

It lies in that concave chair we saved from the flying saucer day and night and says nothing, which also raises frightening questions.

Is it mute? Is it simply ignorant of human speech? Is it even capable of human speech? Right now, it doesn't even seem to have lungs, much less a throat or mouth. Or is it watching and waiting?

If this thing from the stars is sentient, do its thought processes parallel human thought?

Just as frightening and unknown is how Army Intelligence will handle this.

There seem to be only a few real choices. They can wash their hands of everything and destroy the creature. They'll do that over my dead body. Or they can eventually give America the blunt truth...not likely. Or they can make Staloone just another in a string of lies.

Stripped to the bone, the real truth is that we don't know what we're doing. There is no precedent to follow. At this point, it seems that we have discovered a new species of animal that isn't created by or subject to the physical laws of earth.

•••

Eric folded the newspaper carefully, and threw it on the carpeted floor. He picked up the glass from the little table, and drained it of rum. Then he slumped in his chair, and closed the heavy lids of his eyes.

That's when he heard the knock on his door.

He knew it couldn't possibly be anyone but Jimmie, so he said, "What do you want, Jimmie? I'm too tired to gab."

But there was no answer.

He was certain that it couldn't be reporters; none had found him since he'd been sent to the hellhole called *Route 66 Western Motel* days ago. So he wearily pushed himself up out of the chair and took his good old time to walk to the door.

At the door, he said, "Jimmie, what do you want? I'm not opening the door until you answer me."

There was no answer. So he opened the door anyway.

The gigantic maggot that stood in the doorway, swaying slightly, had a mouth full of fangs where no mouth should be and, standing on its hindquarters, was still as tall as Eric.

It was wearing a beautiful white wedding gown complete with a veil.

It said, *"Are you ready to dance, baby?"*

Gaines raised the gun that had suddenly appeared in his hand and pumped twenty two bullets in the maggot's body.

Then Eric woke up.

CHAPTER FORTY
WEDNESDAY, DEC. 18TH, 11:34PM 1996
TULSA OKLAHOMA UNDISCLOSED LOCATION

The man with the furrowed face said, "Get out."

Another man, nervous and much younger, in a neatly pressed NIAR uniform standing in the hotel doorway said, "I'm sorry. I don't know what else to say."

Having given his final report, he turned, stepped through the doorway, and closed the door behind him.

Saying nothing, his breathing broken and shallow, Toren Walker sat by himself in one of two black, leather chairs in the plush living room of the luxury suite in the Doubletree Hotel. A lamp imitating the Tiffany style sat on his right side on an end table next to his chair. An expensive, half-smoked cigar was still smoking in an ash tray on the table. Walker was wearing a pair of black slacks with a white shirt; its long sleeves, typically rolled up to his elbows, were rolled down to his wrists and buttoned there. His glass of bourbon, straight, was in his left hand. The lamp threw a cone of hazy, yellow light around him in the otherwise dark room.

The weak light did nothing to obscure Walker's dead eyes.

He whispered, "Well, hell," in a small voice not intended to be heard by anyone but himself. He raised his right arm and turned his wrist up and looked at his wristwatch.

Then he slammed his wrist, watch down, on the little table, almost knocking the ash tray and cigar off.

He drew his wrist back and looked at the broken face of the watch.

He said, "It's later than I thought."

After he said it, he opened the small drawer in the end table, took out a hand gun, and laid it down on the little table. Toren closed the drawer.

He chuckled.

He took a sip of the bourbon, transferred the glass to his right hand, then placed it next to the hand gun. He picked up the gun.

Toren placed the barrel of the hand gun next to his right temple. Then he whispered the name of the one person that he hated most in his life, the one person that he hated even more than he hated himself.

He said, "Celeste."

And pulled the trigger.

THURSDAY, JANUARY 16, 10:02AM, 1996
TULSA OKLAHOMA LOCATION CLASSIFIED

His suit was dirty and wrinkled as if he had slept in it because he had, and he wore the gray stubble of three days without shaving on his chin.

He was Larry Odom but he wasn't; he wasn't carrying his trademark attaché case either as he paced back and forth and said, "For God's sake, get up off of the floor and get dressed.

"We're going to see Celeste."

But Sslits did not get up off of the bare, concrete floor where the alien lay. It was watching *Sesame Street* on the little television in the room where the alien and its lawyer had been sequestered under protective custody because of the furor over the Battle in the Brady that had seized and outraged Tulsa's imagination.

Sslits was lying on the floor watching the twenty inch television sitting on a cheap television stand because the alien's massive weight would have shattered the one couch or either of the two chairs in the Spartan room into kindling. The alien's Fedora and overcoat were draped over the back of one of those chairs; its big boots sat unlaced on its seat.

Their cramped quarters were not in a hotel or in a city or county jail cell, or anywhere that Odom recognized as a legal restraint for himself or his alien client. That they were not in a city or county jail cell and already under arrest and awaiting trial was due entirely to Odom's journeyman job of creating the most convoluted and often contradictory web of suits, countersuits, briefs, position papers and restraints in the history of American jurisprudence. Of that, he was justly proud.

For days, Odom had felt like he had been ankle-deep in a herd of questions without answers heading off of a cliff like lemmings. Today was no different.

He still did not know why Main Street had been littered with dead bodies or who had turned those once living people into corpses. He had no earthly knowledge of the horror that looked like the Indian Goddess of Death...not what is was, not where it came from, and not why it was in the Brady District of downtown Tulsa. He also didn't know jack squat about the two thick, twisted black sticks that spit destruction and death and were obviously weapons, or where they were now, or how Eric came to be aiming one of them at Sslits.

He did not know who alerted the police.

He assumed the police had called the nearest fire department that had arrived only minutes later.

He did not know how he was going to defend the indefensible or how many civil lawsuits over damaged property he faced, or even if he was going to end up defending Sslits for murder.

The only two things that he was certain of were how Wood had found them in the Tribune building, that was obvious, and why Eric Gaines was there. But he did not know how Eric knew to be there as the K'huprician horror marched down Main Street with death in its blank eyes to the Tribune building.

His two knowns weren't nearly enough to stop the bleeding of the ulcers in his stomach.

Odom turned and glanced at the television as he paced. The two puppets called Muppets, Bert and Ernie, were discussing math and numbers for the benefit of preschool children. He glanced at Sslits. The alien's blank eyes were riveted to the television screen.

"Damn," Larry cursed. "What a sorry day this is for poor little Larry Odom. On top of everything else, the NIAR has re-filed papers for ownership of you, buddy. What do you think of that, eh? Are you even listening to me?"

Both of the questions were rhetorical and one of the reasons his ulcers were bleeding.

"When the owners of those buildings find out where we are, and they will, they'll be breaking down the door demanding restitution for the damages you and that other 'thing' did to downtown Tulsa. Will you please tell me how I'm supposed to stop that?"

Without taking its gaze off of Bert and Ernie, Sslits hissed, big girls don't cry.

Odom pulled an opened envelope out of the breast pocket of his shirt and said, "So, we're back to that song lyrics sham again, are we? You're nothing but a parrot, is that right? Listen, buddy, I know you can understand every word I say."

He waved the envelope in his left hand in the air.

"And if the property damages aren't enough to crush me to dust, there's this little jewel that the police gave me this morning with breakfast."

As he continued to pace, Odom opened the envelope, took the letter out, and scanned its contents quickly.

"It's a registered letter from Celeste's ex-husband, Eric Gaines.

"You'd think an alien from outer space was the biggest diamond in the world. Now Eric is staking an ownership claim on you, too. Not that I'm surprised."

On the television screen, Bert said, "One plus one equals two, Ernie."

"Wow, Bert, who told you that?"

"Count Von Count, you silly goose."

"Hey," objected Ernie, "I'm not a silly goose. That hurt my feelings, Bert."

Odom continued, "I know that's what I'm banking on, buddy, that you're the biggest most valuable damn diamond in the solar system. Her diaries alone have made us a small fortune. The problem with that, of course, is that we are in desperate need of a big fortune."

Larry stopped beside Sslits, his hands on his hips, and glared down at the alien.

"Of course, there's that other little thing you do. That little magic routine. After a little dip in you, I saw her switch from being seventy years old to being thirty as easy as most people change underwear. Of course, now I know you can't fix everything."

Sslits watched as Count Von Count joined Bert and Ernie on the screen. The vampiric puppet said, "Goood Evening! Did I hear someone say that addition sucks?"

Odom continued, "The home office tells me to forget your scientific value. According to the law firm of McCormick Eaton Myers and Odom— kindly notice the last name—you're a freakin' fountain of youth and a gold mine all wrapped up in one big bowl of jello!"

Count Von Count raised one hand with one finger extended. He drawled, "Ernie is right, Bert. One…" he held up his other hand with one finger extended. "And one do make two."

Larry threw up both of his hands in exasperation, the Gaines letter forgotten in his left hand. In imitation of Count Von Count and Odom,

Sslits held up both of its hands with all of its eight pseudo-fingers extended.

Ignoring the alien, Odom added, "Not that you know death from doughnuts...but we're going to visit Celeste. I'm not going to tell you again. Get up and get dressed. Your clothes are in the chair over there.

The lawyer shook his head in disbelief as the alien struggled up on its knees. "God knows why but she did love you!" He walked to the television set and turned it off.

Sslits burbled, *TWOS.*

Odom stared at the alien's hands. Five fingers were extended. The lawyer said, "Damn. In a world where nothing is black or white, you give gray a bad name."

He held up the first two fingers of his right hand.

"This is two, you big, sniveling idiot."

Sslits nodded its head and said, *fives.*

Underneath its back-blown shock of faux hair, the alien that now looked like Count Von Count held up four of its faux fingers.

Odom spread his fingers and thumbs and shook them in the alien's face.

"No, No, No, you moron! This many is five. This many. Now, go get dressed!!!

Sslits gurgled Ones.

CHAPTER FORTY ONE
LOCATION CLASSIFIED

Larry Odom said, "Watch where you step, Sslits. Show at least a little respect, will yah?"

Odom was dressed in his best suit. He had shaved and he carried a little garden trowel in his left hand and Celeste's last journal in his right hand.

It was mid-afternoon and a beautiful day under a cloudless, cerulean blue sky, as he and Sslits walked slowly down the manicured lawn to see Celeste. Except for the twenty or so federal and military agents and local police men who followed at a respectable distance, i.e. within range to shoot Odom, Sslits, or any unauthorized intruder in the back, the meticulously green lawn was empty and eerily silent. It seemed that even no birds sang from the branches of the carefully spaced and manicured trees and they were far enough away from the road that even the sounds of cars and trucks and motorcycles were suppressed.

Sslits was dressed in the same bulky overcoat, huge construction workers steel-toed boots, and an equally oversized slouch hat that the alien had worn in what seemed like a million years ago at the Eastland Mall. Beneath his Fedora, he looked like Ronald Reagan.

When the lawyer reached the foot of a newly turned mound of earth, Odom simply said, "Stop, Sslits; we're here."

To his great surprise and relief, Sslits stopped.

Before Odom opened Celeste's little black book, and as they stood quietly on the sward like two of the biggest morons the world had ever seen, Odom thought *who's the bigger idiot, me or it; I pulled every string in the book to make this happen for a blob that doesn't even know...*but he couldn't bring himself to finish the thought because he knew he was really doing this for himself anyway. The truth be known, Celeste Gaines was the only woman he had ever loved. If she had been wrong about most of the decisions she'd made, at least she was certainly right about that. So instead of saying out loud what he thought, he opened Celeste's journal to the pages he wanted to read by using a thumb as a bookmark and said:

"I don't really completely understand why I'm doing this, Celeste. I never have cared for rituals or ceremonies, but it just felt like I needed to do something since we couldn't come...they wouldn't allow us to come to the earlier ceremony."

His voice caught. He stopped speaking for a silent moment and turned his face away from Sslits to calm his emotions. Then he turned back to face the mound and continued.

"I don't even know who I'm doing this for since, as you know better than anyone else, this giant piece of slobber standing next to me has no idea what I'm doing. But, well, I really felt like this thing and I should do something, so I just brought myself, and it, and your last journal. I'm going to read something out of it, the last entry. That seems appropriate and at least seems meaningful to me. So, here goes."

He raised the journal level with his face and began to read.

Journal. Celeste Gaines. July 1996.

If I have learned anything in my life, it is that the whole world is sick with lies. Everyone lies. We lie about aging, about death and about power. We lie about sex, turning it into the only fantasy that most men or women can hope to fulfill.

We lie to everyone, to those we love, and about love. And we deceive ourselves that we deceive others, that we even deceive God.

I know because I am the worst liar of all.

Because I didn't fall into Sslits the first time. I jumped.

I intentionally jumped into a horror of a writhing, self-contained, sentient, communal mass of cellular maggots in a bladder of hard-water, mad, I thought originally, with ravenous, flesh tearing, squirming thirst. When I learned better— when I realized that the maggots were Sslits—I jumped into that repulsive nightmare of mucous to learn everything that I had failed to learn about the alien through endless, and fruitless experimentation. What I learned was that the maggots knew I jumped. What I learned next might have saved me four decades of pain and degradation if I'd just reported it. But I didn't. I lied.

My very first lie to my superiors damned me. It was a lie of omission. I knew Sslits was the vanguard of an invasion of Earth, and I told no one. The things had obviously failed as proven by the other dead aliens in the crater, so why bother? I didn't think anyone would believe me either, but that's just an excuse, a lie to myself.

My second lie damned us all.

Since that first jump, I've known all the maggots would know everything that Sslits had learned about Earth Seven the instant Sslits touched another Hive...about a planet ripe for invasion. And I knew another woudl come, 'brother' of the first. In an hour. In ten years. In a thousand, they would come.

And I told no one because I knew that Sslits would be destroyed, and no scientist on Earth would ever even think of destroying the greatest breakthrough in cosmic knowledge in human history.

I also lied because I believed in something bigger than me despite my own doubts. Maybe not the Baptist something they taught me in Byng, but something. Something that created the universe, the immutable laws of gravity, of time, of energy and mass. That something that I had struggled to believe in for too long, that created me. And Sslits. And everything.

I believed that the Laws of morality were just as universal as the Laws of gravity and time and energy and mass. I believed that they were absolute laws on Earth and Mars and K'hupric.

Laws that control the lives of all sentient creatures.

I still believe it even though I don't believe it. Nuts, huh?

•••

Odom stopped reading for a moment to glance at the alien at his side. Its attention seemed riveted to the headstone above the grave, its fingers steepled and then unsteepled and then steepled again like a child makes and unmakes the roof of a church. Odom shook his head no in disappointment, then continued to read:

Yes, there were reasons that lead me to my conclusions.

Initially, the NIAR classified Sslits as 'incapable of thought independent of its biological programming; a totally instinctive animal'. I knew that wasn't true.

Later, Wood reported Sslits 'barely able to parrot human words.'
Sure.

Barely capable of piloting a starship billions of miles across space. I knew better than that also.

I refused to believe that morality isn't universal. Or that communication could not erase what separated Sslits from me. I could not believe that. I would not believe it.

And that I nor anyone else could not change what God had made.
I would change Sslits.

Forty-eight years. Forty-eight years of failure. I didn't change one iota of what God had made...not one jot or title of the thing called Sslits.

But even fools can learn.

I feel almost clean now. The truth has set me free.

Sslits is no more than a mindless alien parrot.

These will be the last words I record in my Journal.

There will also be no more alien baths. Thatt lie is ended and I suspect my return to my actual age may even kill me. But I'm doing it anyway. We'll see.

Tomorrow, I will relinquish Sslits back into Toren's custody. Tomorrow, the NIAR learns about monsters and invasions, and the truth about me.

I have sinned against myself....against man....
And against God.

And I know with utmost certainty that the wages of my sin is death.
Mine.

Odom looked to his right at Sslits, standing as if the lawyer had said and done nothing, with its faux fingers steepled in front of its face. Odom returned to the journal and read:

I'm a big girl and I'll take whatever comes. I know that I must face

*this by myself, that I must stand alone, and stand holding on to what my
grandmother said: when things seem utterly hopeless...*

    One, with God, is a majority.

Odom closed the diary and knelt in the grass next to the fresh mound
of earth.

He laid the little black book on the edge of that mound and, being
careful not to soil it, he dug a small hole in the dirt with his trowel.

Then he placed the journal in the hole, and covered it with dirt.

He stood up and brushed the dirt from the knees of his pants. He looked
to his right at the alien, still standing at the foot of Celeste's headstone
with its fingers steepled. Its blank eyes were still fixed on the tombstone.

The dates beneath her name on the headstone read Oct. 20, 1916 and
Nov. 26, 1996.

He said, "You wrote that you hadn't accomplished a thing, not a single
change in the bag of mucous standing next to me, and I guess that's
true. So you were wrong to even try, maybe, but you sure changed—" he
struggled to finish the thought "—you sure changed me."

And, for the first time, although he had known it as a fact in his head,
Larry accepted, embraced, that Celeste was indeed dead, and that he
would never hold the woman he loved in his arms, or hear her laugh that
silly little laugh again, or see that unyielding look on her face when she
knew that she was right, and he began to cry.

And as he cried, he looked at Sslits.

Sslits, unhuman, its hands at its side and the face beneath its blown-
back sheaf of hair Celeste's face, whispered, *one.*

EPILOGUE

It was the dead of night. A gibbous, yellow moon hung in the black sky
splattered with stars. There were no clouds. The silence was oppressive
in the unnatural round clearing burned in the middle of a heavy copse
of trees in sparsely populated north Tulsa. Spashs flying saucer sat in the
middle of the clearing. A black van was parked at its edge.

The van had been parked for some time close to a ramp that descended
from the huge, silver, flying saucer in the center of the circle. But the
ramp had been drawn up seamlessly into the side of the spaceship. The
van's headlights were dark; no glint of light randomly flashed from those

headlights or even from the moon above on the spaceship's highly polished skin. The teeth of the circular dome in the center of the spacecraft looked somewhat like the mid-span supports in a jet engine.

No breeze stirred the trees around the flying saucer, no birds sang or insects chirruped.

It was a dead zone.

The now-sealed mouth in its skin opened inside onto a perfectly smooth, circular hallway that seemed to constantly and endlessly curve deeper into the spaceship. It was impossible to tell if its walls were organic or inorganic, and it was well lit but by no discernible source of light. The oppressive heat on the skin of the craft when it initially landed in the copse was absent from its bowels. Eerie silence and an oppressive feeling of claustrophobia permeated the tunnel.

A fork in the hall curved to the left and to the right.

One tube opened onto the center of the K'huprician cockpit where, under a chaos of disconnected cables and wires, a silver concave seat stood.

Seated on the pilot's chair was an unspeakable horror, almost unhuman, his head resting on his chest. His broken sobs violated the otherwise dead silence in the cockpit and for a distance out into the connecting hallway.

Leprosy had eaten his nose, an ear, and three fingers. Limp strands of hair hung from an otherwise scarred, bald skull, and angry red nodules checker-boarded an otherwise fish-belly white face and dead skin.

He slowly lifted his head from his chest and, although there were tears in his red-rimmed eyes, he chuckled.

His chuckles escalated into laugher, and that laughter intensified, racking his body.

He smiled as he laughed and his upper rotted lip curled up exposing a top row of ragged, yellowed teeth as he did so.

His laughter rose in pitch and volume and began to echo.

Madness burned in his eyes.

THE END

APPENDIX A

Excerpts from N.I.A.R. confidential files

[Compiled from experiments conducted from 1947—1971 and from information (often unconfirmed and *open to suspicion*) submitted by ex-agent, Celeste Gaines.]

Sslits (codename: B.L.O.O.D.T.I.D.E.)
Height: maximum, 30' elongated; humanoid height, 6'5"   Weight: approximately 300 gallons
Hair: none Eyes: none (pseudo eyes while humanoid)
Sex: none (vaguely male while humanoid
Birth date: unknown   Age: unknown; Sslits is very old
Birthplace: a desolate planet in another galaxy called K'hupric; location unclear
Current N.I.A.R. status: under guardianship of ex-N.I.A.R. agent, Celeste Gaines, pending court action.

Physical & Mental Abilities

Sslits (approximation of unpronounceable name) is composed of liquids unknown of Earth. The alien's 'skin' is a thin layer of these liquids hardened to maintain a humanoid shape (a late development). It is hideous in its natural state, most like a giant amoeba. Punctured, this skin reseals almost instantly except for major ruptures, and is amazingly malleable. Sslits can change to almost any form and can stretch to a height of about 30 feet before its body ruptures.

Sslits is ancient by human standards, but not immortal; extremely powerful, but not invincible. It is terrified by large bodies of water like a lake, river or ocean because extended immersion would cause dissolution. Even a heavy rainstorm could destroy the alien.

Every drop of expended liquid must be replenished, or Sslits will perish. It absorbs liquid from the air at all times: people around it always feel thirsty. This absorption was how Sslits and the race fed on K'hupric, its planet of origin.

In addition, it can absorb such great amounts of any liquid into its body by immersing part of its body into the source. New infusions do not compromise the primary composition of its chemical nature, but certain tested liquids have affected the alien in ways undiscoverable to current scientific processes. Some can poison, even kill. Sslits is not familiar with most liquids on Earth; this attribute is dissuaded.

It can morph parts of itself into a waterspout or thin and powerful stream of water. Using pseudo legs as hydraulic jets, it can leap tremendous distances (measured at 150'). An arm turned into a waterspout becomes a terrific ram, or can suffocate a human subject into unconsciousness or drown when forced into mouth and nostrils.

Troubling is an unconfirmed reported ability to physically and mentally meld through immersion into its body, accomplished only by Celeste Gaines. Both human physical rejuvenation and healing, and a mental communication impossible on a human level is suspected.

Sslits' K'huprician societal structure sounds like "Hive" to the human ear in its hissing tongue, and equivocates the seemingly shared consciousness and purpose of communal insects like ants and bees. Born for its inescapable Hive position, Sslits is incapable of independent thought and action outside the limits of instinct and its own nature. Its primary instinct is survival.

Most troubling, Sslits speaks human words. As with chimpanzees, evidence is not conclusive on whether it comprehends their meanings. Because most utterances seem inappropriate to their situations, the majority consensus is that Sslits simply parrots sound.

Sslits seems to have no concept of morality understood on any human level.

Conclusion: Sslits remains a creature of unfathomable paradox.

ABOUT OUR CREATORS

AUTHOR –

MICHAEL VANCE - was born in Oklahoma City, Oklahoma. He was first published in "The Professor's Story Hour" chapbook at the age of eleven. He has been published in dozens of magazines and as a syndicated columnist and cartoonist in over 500 newspapers. His history book, *Forbidden Adventures, The History of the American Comics Group*, has been called a "benchmark in comics history". It was reprinted in *Alter Ego* magazine #s 61 & 62.

His magazine work has been published in seven countries, and includes articles for *Starlog, Jack & Jill* and *Star Trek, The Next Generation*.

He briefly ghosted the internationally syndicated comic strip, *Alley Oop*, and created and wrote his own strip for five years called *Holiday Out* that was reprinted as a comic book. Vance also wrote comic book titles including *Straw Men, Angel of Death, The Adventures of Captain Nemo, Holiday Out* and *Bloodtide*. Artists with whom he has worked include, Wayne Truman, Richard "Grass" Green, and Dave (Alley Oop) Graue.

His work has appeared in several comic book anthologies, and he is listed in two reference works, the *Who's Who of American Comic Books* and *Comic Book Superstars*.

His thirty short stories about a fictional town called "Light's End" have been published in numerous magazines. They have also been recorded by legendary actor William (*Murder She Wrote*) Windom. One of these stories was nominated for the international 2004 SLF Fountain Award for Best Short Story.

These short stories were the foundation for a trilogy of novels published by Airship 27: *Weird Horror Tales, Weird Horror Tales: The Feasting*, and *Weird Horror Tales: Light's End*.

With novelists Mel Odom and R.A. Jones, he co-wrote *Global Star*, a tabloid in a world where werewolves and babies born with bowling balls in their stomachs are reality.

He co-wrote *The Equation*, a suspense-thriller about the impending financial collapse of America, with R. A. Jones, and *Motor City Manhunt*, a crime novel set in Detroit in the 1930s.

Snake: Nest of Vipers was inspired by an unpublished synopsis possibly from the 1950 written by comics pioneer Richard E. Hughes.

Airship 27 also published Vance's novel, *Young Nemo and the Black Knights* about Jules Vern's Captain Nemo as a young man of eighteen years of age.

The Thief of Two Worlds is Vance's first middle grade, Christian SF novel about a trip back into time to recover a 'jewel' of infinite value. *All In Color for a Time* is its sequel.

Vance's weekly comics review column, *Suspended Animation*, was continuously published for more than twenty years in fanzines, newspapers, and on over eighty websites. At its peak, it was read by approximately 4,000,000 readers a year. It was the longest, continuously published, comics review column in the world.

In his career, he worked in newspapers for twenty-two years as an editor, writer and advertising manager, creating three successful newspaper magazines. He also worked as an advertising copy writer, journalist, novelist, historian, graphic designer, in public relations, as a grant writer, cartoonist and columnist.

Vance also created the Oklahoma Cartoonists Collection housed in the Toy and Action Figure Museum in Pauls Valley, Oklahoma, and was a keynote speaker at the "Uncanny Adventures of Okie Cartoonists" exhibit at the Oklahoma Historical Museum in Oklahoma City He is a Christian.

INTERIOR ILLUSTRATOR –

GARY KATO – was born in Honolulu, in 1949. He graduated from the University of Hawaii with a Bachelor in Fine Arts degree. His comic book work has appeared in such varied titles as Destroyer Duck, Thunderbunny, Ms. Tree and Mr. Jigsaw. He's also illustrated children's books such as The Menehune of Naupaka Village and the currently available Barry Baskerville Returns and Jamie and the Fish-Eyed Goggles. He's also been a contributor to the Children's Television Workshop magazines, 3-2-1 Contact and Kid City.

COVER ARTIST –

TED HAMMOND - is a Canadian artist who has been creating amazing art for over twenty years. His work has appeared in magazines, ads, books and graphic novels just to name a few. Go to (www.tedhammond.com) to contact him and check out more of his work!

•••

My special thanks to my dear friend and sometimes coauthor, R. A. Jones, for plot input on *Sslits* so many, many years ago.

Other books by Michael Vance available from Airship 27:

Motor City Manhunt (with R.A. Jones)
ISBN-13: 978-0692622766
ISBN-10: 0692622764

Snake: Nest of Vipers
ISBN-13: 978-0692406472
ISBN-10: 0692406476

Young Nemo and the Black Knights
ISBN-13: 978-0692340165
ISBN-10: 0692340165

Weird Horror Tales trilogy:
Weird Horror Tales
ISBN-13: 978-0615807782
ISBN-10: 061580778X

Weird Horror Tales: The Feasting
ISBN-13: 978-0615889047
ISBN-10: 0615889042

Weird Horror Tales: Light's End
ISBN-13: 978-0615889047
ISBN-10: 0615889042

Also by Michael Vance:

www.ingramcontent.com/pod-product-compliance
Lightning Source LLC
Chambersburg PA
CBHW051127260626
47170CB00005B/1698